HEROES
AGAINST ALL ODDS

Illinois

VIVIAN LEIBER

Safety of His Arms

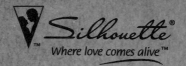

Silhouette®

Where love comes alive™

9 780373 822119

ISBN 0-373-82211-1

50450

Illinois
State Facts

Nickname:	Land of Lincoln
Date Entered Union:	December 3, 1818 (the 21st state)
Motto:	State sovereignty, national union
Illinois Men:	Jimmy Connors, *tennis player* Miles Davis, *musician* Walt Disney, *film animator, producer* Ronald Reagan, *former U.S. president* Sam Shepard, *playwright*
Flower:	Purple Violet
Bird:	Cardinal
Fun Fact:	The world's first skyscraper was built in Chicago, 1885.

FRITZ'S BEDTIME PRAYER:

Dear God,

I've tried to be the bestest boy for my mommy, but sometimes it's hard. I know she's sad sometimes, and so am I since Daddy died. But I think Daddy sent Sensei Logan to be our guardian angel. He's the biggest, baddest angel I ever seen, but he makes Mommy and me feel safe. And he makes Mommy and me smile. I hope Sensei Logan stays around for a long, long, long, long time.

American HEROES
AGAINST ALL ODDS

VIVIAN LEIBER

Safety of His Arms

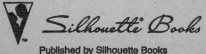

Silhouette Books

Published by Silhouette Books
America's Publisher of Contemporary Romance

This book is dedicated
to Alice Orr

SILHOUETTE BOOKS
300 East 42nd St.,
New York, N. Y. 10017

ISBN 0-373-82211-1

SAFETY OF HIS ARMS

About the Author

Vivian Leiber lives in Winnetka, Illinois, a town with three stoplights, one doctor, seven churches, one public school, two parks...and only one hero she's interested in: her husband. Vivian writes stories that make us laugh, make us cry, make us remember what it's like to fall in love, and they help us to while away a few hours in a world in which happy endings are never more than a few pages away.

Books by Vivian Leiber

Silhouette Romance

Casey's Flyboy #822
Goody Two-Shoes #871
Her Own Prince Charming #896
Safety of His Arms #1070
The Bewildered Wife #1237
The 6'2", 200 lb. Challenge #1292
Soldier and the Society Girl #1358
The Marriage Merger #1366

Harlequin American Romance

Baby Makes Nine #576
Blue-Jeaned Prince #640
Marrying Nicky #655
A Million-Dollar Man #672
Always A Hero #686
An Ordinary Day #712
Secret Daddy #761
One Sexy Daddy #792

Harlequin Intrigue

His Kind of Trouble #416
His Betrothed #460

Dear Reader,

It happens every day, on street corners and in coffee shops, front porch stoops and church socials. A woman opens her heart...to a hero. True-blue everyday American heroes live on either coast, in small towns and big-city lofts, on farms and in suburban cul-de-sacs. They do remarkable things on otherwise unremarkable days. They're the men who rescue the cat from the neighbor's tree (again!), talk the nervous teen through a first driver's license test, brave a fire to rescue a child, change a tire for a stranded motorist. "Just doing my job," they'll say—all the while thinking that every man would do the same. Never realizing the truth—that not every man is a hero.

When you open this book, you'll be meeting one of my favorite heroes. Logan Powell, a former cop, is not afraid of the bullet or the brawl. But he is afraid...to love. And Trish Eastman—I hope you like her, too! She's a woman just like you and me. Watch her open her heart to this hero— and come into the *Safety of His Arms*.

Have a wonderful read!

Vivian Leiber

Please address questions and book requests to:
Silhouette Reader Service
U.S.: 3010 Walden Ave., P.O. Box 1325, Buffalo, NY 14269
Canadian: P.O. Box 609, Fort Erie, Ont. L2A 5X3

Chapter One

"**Y**ou know, when you think about it—a jumping jack is a pretty hard thing to learn."

Trish Eastman looked up from her newspaper at the woman seated next to her on the bleachers. A very typical Hubbard Woods mother, she wore a purple T-shirt over black leggings and her hair was pulled back in a no-nonsense ponytail. Trish thought she looked familiar, maybe a mom to one of Fritz's kindergarten classmates.

"I mean, think about how the kids have to learn to coordinate their arms and their feet and then add the jumping," the woman added. "If taking my Paul to karate class twice a week can teach him how to do one of them, then I guess it's worth it.''

Trish nodded, trying to look really interested.

"My name's Krysia Miller," the woman said. "My Paul is the third one from the end, there on the left, rubbing his eyes like he's about to take a nap. We met once before at the kindergarten orientation meeting, but I'm afraid I've completely forgotten your name."

Trish introduced herself and looked at the lineup of twenty-odd five-year-olds dressed in the traditional white karate *gi*. Pointing out her own son was easy, since Fritz had a crop of carrot-colored hair which stood out in any crowd. Trish had to suppress the urge to walk across the gym to yet again roll up the legs of his pants. Glancing more closely at the others, she stifled a smile. The boy to Fritz's right distractedly sucked his thumb, while a boy to her son's left was obviously lost in a daydream, his eyes drooping.

The students faced the community house *sensei*, a broad-shouldered man who moved gracefully through the deceptively simple moves necessary for a jumping jack.

Hands stretch high above the head. Hands come back to rest by your hips. The feet, spread apart one moment and then touching together the next.

And, oh, yes, the jumping.

Putting it all together wasn't easy, and within seconds of trying to copy their master, some of the boys were struck with a serious case of the giggles. But before it had a chance to infect the entire class, the lesson moved on to a series of defenses and punches against an imaginary attacker.

In each movement of the instructor, Trish sensed a power tightly and scrupulously reined in for the purposes of teaching the youngsters—like a lion demonstrating the predatory craft for cubs. As her eyes traveled from his bare feet to the uppermost blond curl on his head, with several involuntary lingering pauses along the way, Trish felt an unbidden, unexpected reminder that she was a woman.

As subtle and as quiet as a whisper, it was a stir of attraction that came and went in an instant. Caught up in it, Trish didn't hear her own soft exclamation.

"I was wondering how long it would take before you'd notice him," Krysia said. "He's amazing, isn't he?"

Trish felt a quick, hot blush on her face.

"I wasn't even thinking about..." she protested. "Well, okay, maybe I was."

"Hey, I wouldn't mind having Sensei Logan Powell protect me from the, uh, elements," Krysia said, fluttering her lashes with a sensuality borrowed from Mae West.

"Krysia, I'm shocked!" Trish exclaimed with mock horror.

The woman directly in front of them on the bleachers turned around and slapped Krysia's knee playfully.

"She promised to love, honor and cherish Michael Miller. She didn't say anything about not looking. And, you've got to admit, Logan Powell's definitely a looker."

A ripple of giggles infected the other mothers seated on the bleachers.

Krysia poked Trish suggestively.

"I seem to remember that you're single," she said. "*I* can only look, but *you* can do something about it."

Trish felt the slightest tremor of self-consciousness mixed with pain.

Yes, she was single now—and it felt like she'd been deported to a foreign territory. So many years of assuming that she would be Mrs. Robert Eastman forever....

"I might be single, but I'm very much out of practice," she quipped lightly.

A hoot of laughter followed.

Right then, for the briefest moment, Trish felt a part of things, as if she really belonged to the group of Hubbard Woods mothers. Technically, of course, she already belonged.

She was a mother.

She lived in Hubbard Woods.

She'd been living here four months, since she'd carefully backed the rented moving truck into the alley behind the Hubbard Woods pharmacy.

So, she was a Hubbard Woods mother, right?

But becoming a real part of the community had been a lot harder than moving what furniture she had up the narrow stairs to the second floor apartment overlooking the cobblestone parking lot.

Four months later and she still felt as if she would never quite fit in with the breezily self-confident mothers she met. They all seemed to know each other from high school, greeted each other at the nursery school door at noon pickup as if they were bosom buddies, meeting time and again throughout a day of their children's lessons and play dates and birthday parties.

Maybe all their cheerful smiles hid anxieties as palpable as her own. Maybe they weren't really as secure as they seemed. Maybe they had days like Trish still occasionally had, where getting up out of bed was an act of courage.

But she had a tough time persuading herself of that.

For this space in time, sharing smiles and womanly mischief while ogling the karate instructor, she could forget herself and feel only the easy camaraderie of suburban motherhood.

They had let her in. And Krysia Miller's offhand introduction was like a gift from God.

The conversation drifted around her as Krysia was drawn by the woman in front of them into a conversation about a church men's-group outing the previous week. Trish felt the return of her isolation. She went back to scanning the newspaper.

Inwardly she reassured herself. It will take time, Trish. It was what she told her son, Fritz, every night.

It will take time, she thought to herself once again. In so many ways, for so many things, it will take time. It was hard to learn how to do a jumping jack and it was hard to learn how to fit in. But it *would* happen.

"Ohmigosh, trouble," Krysia said, jarring Trish out of her mental pep talk.

Trish looked up from her newspaper. Without her glasses it was hard to tell, but she could see that the lesson had come to an unnatural standstill. The class was at rigid attention. Trish squinted her eyes and saw Fritz standing on the sidelines, separate from his classmates, his head ducked down over his chest.

"We do not fight in this class," Logan Powell was saying sternly.

His steel-laced words had brought an abrupt end to his students' fidgeting, daydreaming, thumb sucking and uniform tugging. Even the mothers had now stopped their conversations midsentence, and they remained in uneasy silence as they watched the unfolding drama.

Although Trish hadn't seen what had happened, she could feel Fritz's humiliation as he stood with bowed head at the sidelines. The natural urge to protect her son welled up within her and was transformed into a distinct sense of not liking this Logan Powell. It didn't matter that she had admired him only minutes before. He was obviously directing his words to her baby.

"Karate is *not* about hurting others," the *sensei* explained in a rough voice. "It is about protecting yourself from others who are stupid enough to want to fight.''

Trish leaned forward and her heart shuddered as she watched her son close his eyes. Oh, no, she thought. Feeling a catch in her own throat, she wondered if he would begin to cry.

To have this happen to him, to be singled out on his very first day of class, on top of everything else he faced!

''Fritz was wrong to punch another boy,'' Logan was saying, looking hard at each member of the class. ''Now he will have to sit on the sidelines for five minutes.''

At this point, Fritz turned around, stealing a look toward the bleachers, searching for the familiar sight of his mother. Trish hesitantly raised her hand, hoping she could catch his eye. If only she could communicate some of the fierce love she had for him....

''Fritz, you will spend that five minutes watching the class!'' the *sensei* barked, and Fritz jerked back to attention. ''If you do not, you will not be allowed back into class at all.''

Fritz's face, already pink, got redder.

She hadn't been able to make contact with her son, hadn't even, with a wave or an encouraging smile, been able to tell him that all would be well. A surge of anger, familiar only to a parent, surged through her. It didn't matter what her boy had done.

This Sensei Logan Powell, with his last command, had taken from her a mother's prerogative to comfort.

"Is that your son?" the woman in front of her asked sympathetically, turning to look up at Trish.

Trish nodded.

"I wouldn't put up with that," she declared self-righteously.

Trish felt torn. Perhaps, as a good mother, she *shouldn't* let Fritz be humiliated. Maybe she *should* walk right across the gym, scoop him up in her arms, and walk away. But wouldn't that be even more humiliating for him?

She knew she was too protective of him, but then again, she had every reason for that protectiveness.

If this experience was any indication, however, maybe she should drop karate from his list of activities. But activities—such as "Ice Mice" skating classes, Supersports at the elementary school gym, Saturday morning story time at the library—were the breeding ground for five-year-old friendships.

And God knew her little boy needed friendships. Badly. And Peewee Karate was the most popular of the activities available at the Community House. She had carefully researched this, mindful of what had been happening for so long now. Every night, so painfully she sometimes had to turn away so he wouldn't see her tears, Fritz had said he had no friends.

Though she always told him "But you have me" they both knew that wasn't enough.

Which was why she always counted with him. He *did* have friends. There was Jim, the clerk at the drugstore, who sometimes treated him with an extra piece of gum. There was Kurt, the mailman who let him put the envelopes into the building's individual mailbox slots. And there was Tim, the manager at McDonald's, who remembered everybody's name.

"That was three, four if you counted Mom," she would say softly.

But they both knew that it wasn't enough because it didn't include boys his own age.

Which was why he was here and had to sit at the end of a long line of boys whose faces were an impassive mixture of pity and fear. Pity at his being singled out in anger by the *sensei*. Fear that somehow they, too, would be taken out of class.

Trish swallowed, her heart aching for Fritz. She really had no choice. He had a few tentative friendships now, hard won after months of her driving him to various lessons and activities. There was a kid at skating class who knew his name, a boy at Supersports who let Fritz sit next to him in class. And his kindergarten teacher had said that Fritz was starting to talk to other boys. Trish knew those relationships would blossom.

And she also knew that her little boy had so much to learn.

As painful as it was to watch Fritz sitting forlornly at the sidelines, she knew he had to stick with karate. There wasn't a five-year-old Hubbard Woods boy who wasn't in this class and if Fritz wanted friends—and if she wanted him to be happy—he would have to sit quietly, pay attention and hope to be let back into the class.

"If it were Paul, he wouldn't take it as well as Fritz is," Krysia said in an encouraging whisper. "Fritz seems to be doing really well. He's a tough kid."

Trish watched her son. He didn't move. He didn't squirm.

"I think I'll talk to the teacher after class,"

she said to Krysia, coming to a quick decision. "If I know Fritz, he's going to be ruminating on this for weeks."

And, most likely, crying. And begging to quit karate, as well as ice skating and Supersports and going to the library and going to school and living in Hubbard Woods, for that matter. Sympathy for Fritz mixed with a touch of impending weariness. The next few days were bound to be even rougher than usual.

Though the mothers had been shocked into silence, as the rest of the class continued with their lessons, they returned to their own conversations. There were no further disruptions of Peewee Karate.

But Trish's heart didn't stop pounding and she didn't even try to return her attention to the day's newspaper. She stared at her son, memorizing his every impassive feature, wishing she could communicate strength to him, admiring him for his stoicism.

Fritz remained this way, waiting until the barest nod from Logan made it clear that he had permission to get up. He returned to the end of the lineup and accomplished the remaining exercises with a stubborn determination. At precisely four-thirty, Logan dismissed the class.

The boys shrieked and raced back to their mothers to put on socks and shoes and to argue over whether they would wear their jackets in the early autumn cool.

Fritz ran to Trish and flung himself into her arms and cried, letting loose the emotions he had doggedly kept inside for the past fifteen minutes. All around them, boys whooped and yelled. Mothers pleaded for cooperation and cheery goodbyes were shouted between friends. But Trish could only hear her son's sobs and feel his fingers digging into her arms as he clung to her.

"I'm never coming back to this stupid class!" he cried hoarsely.

Trish wrapped her arms around him and softly stroked his hair. With each sob, she could feel his pain, the pain of the last year—losing his father, moving away from his old neighborhood, feeling like an outsider in Hubbard Woods, and now this.

It was a small thing, compared to everything he had been through in the last year. Small—but not to Fritz. For him, she knew, it was a major blow.

"I don't want to be in karate!" he concluded, hiccuping. "And I don't want to do that stupid story time at the library anymore, and I don't like my school, and I don't..."

Krysia tapped Trish on the shoulder.

"How about if I take the boys to the Sweet Shoppe for a little treat?" she offered.

Instantly, she had Fritz's attention as he looked up, first at her and then at Trish. Then, finally, he glanced at Paul, who stood at Krysia's side.

"Could I, Mom?" he asked. She knew he was wondering if the rules about eating sweets before dinner would be broken, just this once.

Trish hesitated.

"It'll take Fritz's mind off things," Krysia said. "And you could go talk to the instructor without Fritz. You'll feel better. I've gone to bat for my kids lots of times—you need to do the same for yours. Go on, meet us later."

Trish smiled an acceptance, and Fritz's tears dried up. Within seconds, socks and shoes on, he was hand in hand with Paul, bubbling with excitement as they walked out of the gym.

Fritz turned only once to look at his mother, his eyes pink with the residue of tears. Trish's heart melted and determination steeled her spine.

I'm sure if I just talk to the instructor, Trish thought to herself...

* * *

"Hello, I'm Fritz's mother," she said, her voice as steady as she could make it. She approached the *sensei* with a hand extended. "Trish Eastman."

Up close, as he stood reviewing a computer printout listing the boys in his class, Logan Powell was somehow taller and even more intimidating than he had been at the head of the class. Dusty blond hair, deep emerald eyes and muscles that showed every bit of the discipline he had learned in karate. From a distance Trish hadn't seen the tiny but prominent scar beneath his right eye and another, deeper, scar which cut through the center of his chest, but now she noticed both. The latter scar began at the base of his neck and continued until it was covered by the upper folds of his robe.

Briefly, she recalled the light banter about his looks, realizing that her only feeling now was that he possessed an air of masculine confidence which bordered on arrogance.

"You want to talk about Fritz," Logan stated, rather than asked. "You want to tell me that I'm wrong to discipline him."

Trish felt suddenly on the defensive. "I only wanted to ask you to temper the negative you present to Fritz with something positive in the future, because his feelings are so—''

"Listen, lady, this is *my* class. I have to have some discipline here or else these kids will get hurt. Did you see Fritz?''

"No, I didn't,'' Trish admitted, shaking her head. "But even if he was fighting with another boy, maybe just talking to him would be enough. You don't have to humiliate him the way you did.''

As she said the words, she felt her balance return. Logan Powell had taken control of the conversation right from the start. Normally Trish would accede, would listen carefully, would wait for an opening in the conversation *before* trying to make her point. But where her son was concerned, Trish had a reservoir of strength and determination that she herself hadn't fully recognized until now.

She wanted something from this man—something vital for her son. And, regardless of how intimidated she might feel, she had to get him to understand Fritz, to understand what her son needed. He might think she was asking him to completely change the way he taught his class, but all she really wanted was for him to be just a little more sensitive with Fritz. Though he couldn't know what Fritz had been through this past year, she didn't think it was too much to ask for.

It was simple enough, really, and very reasonable, when she thought about it.

"You don't have to shame a five-year-old in order to teach him," she said more forcefully. "Besides, there was another boy—" She faltered momentarily as she remembered that she hadn't actually seen anything, had only become aware of the problem when the gym had gone silent. "The other boy could just as easily be at fault." She had to cross her fingers on that one.

"Fritz wasn't just fighting," Logan corrected. "He punched another boy without any provocation. He was acting out in a way that I can't have in this class."

Trish's heart sank even as she looked away. If that truly was the case, she had no way of refuting his decision. She felt the initiative slipping from her. Nevertheless she tried again.

"All I'm asking is that—"

"You want me to make an exception for your son, Mrs. Eastman. But if I were to do that, I would have every other mother on my back demanding special treatment for theirs," Logan said, interrupting her impatiently. "The world doesn't work like that. In the real world there are rules and a boy like Fritz is going to have to learn that, whether he learns it in my class or elsewhere.''

Logan inwardly flinched, but was determined to stand firm. She wasn't the first Hubbard Woods mother who had come to him after class, but she was the first that had made him pause. While she stood uncertainly in front of him, he tried convincing himself that wasn't why he was being so abrupt with her.

When Trish Eastman had approached him, he had actually had a reaction. The kind of reaction that a man has at the sight of a beautiful woman.

Her hair wasn't "done," he noticed—instead, the waves of dark espresso were pulled back with a simple ribbon that begged, literally begged, to be untied and set free.

The nails weren't manicured, he concluded as he checked for the wedding ring that would have worked like a cold splash of water on his thoughts. Then he found himself fighting back a smile at the chewed-off nails even as he told himself to forget it.

And then there was her face. It wasn't made-up with cosmetics that promised a natural look even while delivering a cold, hardened mask—

although he thought he detected a touch of mascara. Nobody could possibly have such a lush blanket of lashes.

A pretty woman and Logan was simply having the normal reactions of a grown man. A moment of unexpected defenselessness, but then—

Then she opened her mouth and Logan felt everything good and simple and bright about his thoughts dry up.

"There are rules," he found himself saying, his voice more harsh than he'd intended. But he believed every word he said as deeply as he believed in God, in gravity, in the sun rising every morning. He believed in those rules and he couldn't abide those who only agreed to the rules...for everyone else.

"I just can't have fighting in my classroom," he finished. "One of those kids could get hurt out there."

"If you could just temper your words with..."

"I can't change the rules," he said curtly.

At war within herself about whether to confide in this man or not, she said, "But you have to understand Fritz. He's had a rough year."

About to say more, Trish took a closer look at Sensei Powell, and stopped. His unyielding face, his jaw squared with disdain, tipped the balance toward saying nothing more.

"Look, Mrs. Eastman—" He paused, as if he expected her to correct his reference to her marital status. When she said nothing, he continued. "Mrs. Eastman, every kid has a story. First, Johnny should be given extra slack because he has a new sibling. Then, *Jimmy* should be given special treatment because he's a sensitive kid. Then—"

"All right, all right," Trish snapped, interrupting him. She was surprised at the edge in her voice. "This conversation isn't going anywhere."

"That's because you're not getting what you want, lady."

The words, once said, surprised both of them. For her part, Trish was shocked by his intensity. She wondered briefly if he was reacting to things besides her.

Then his strong jaw clenched, his eyes narrowed, and she decided he was, quite simply, a jerk.

"I think that was uncalled for," she said breathlessly, anger lacing her words. "Goodbye."

She turned, resisted the urge to run, and collected her jacket and purse from the bleachers. It was agony not to look back at him, to search for some explanation for his hostility, if not to resolve the problems she faced with Fritz and karate.

"Are you bringing Fritz back?" he called out to her just as she reached the steel exit doors.

She stopped and turned. Thankfully, he was far enough away that he was out of focus, just a blur of muscle and white cotton *gi*. She didn't have to see him, didn't have to beat herself over the head for even that brief moment of attraction that had felt like a betrayal to Robert.

"I don't know," she said honestly. Then she walked out.

Chapter Two

Logan cursed to himself as he shoved his karate uniform into his backpack. He gathered up the *gi*'s black fabric belt into a ball and rammed it in beside the white robe and pants.

He had thought he was immune to mothers who insisted their children were special, to people who believed that rules were meant for others, to "suburbanites" who didn't realize just how tough the real world could be outside the cocoon they built for themselves.

He had gotten accustomed to the idea that people wanted a policeman who would—what was the department motto?—"protect and serve'' and stand in the line of fire *without* support.

Policemen who took the heat for them, time and again. And karate instructors who would make their children black belts without a moment's hard work—as if by osmosis.

Well maybe he hadn't gotten used to the assumptions, but it had certainly stopped surprising him.

Mrs. Eastman had come to him, asking him for...what? He wasn't sure exactly what she had been asking for. All he remembered was the surging irritation at the request for special treatment.

"Change the rules for me and my child."

It was the same request he had heard from others—over and over and over. Yet a small part of him wondered—was that really what she had asked?

After all, thanks to her unknowingly pushing all his buttons, he hadn't really listened. Not *really* listened.

But I'm no chump, he told himself.

She never meant you were, an inner voice reminded him quickly.

He looked up at the floor-to-ceiling mirror of

the locker room, ignoring the masculine features that women seemed to make a fuss over and studying the gnarled scar which ran from the base of his throat down to his rock-hard abdomen. The doctors had done a good job of salvaging the flesh, he thought with careful neutrality, opening up his entire body as if he were an auto to be put back together.

He'd be back on the force in a month, if he was lucky.

A month that felt like a very long time. He wasn't used to spinning his wheels, and had filled up his days with volunteer work until he could come home exhausted for the nights.

The long nights.

As his eyes travelled upward to meet his own in the reflection, he realized the injury to his soul had been something that even the best doctors couldn't repair.

He had come to the realization that there was an optimism to his outlook that had been strained—maybe even destroyed. In that dark street, it had been snuffed out in the roar of gunfire and drowned out by his own scream of pain.

Burnout, that's what they called it.

Lots of cops got it, he knew. That nagging sense that there was nothing left of beauty, kindness and purity in life. But many of those cops left the force.

It wasn't an option for Logan.

Leaving the force was as unthinkable as not breathing, as impossible as stopping the beating of his heart. The force was like a wound that never healed, an itch that always begged for him to scratch, even as the reward that he felt from his work ebbed smaller and weaker with each new day that passed.

He had been on the force since the summer he had graduated from high school, beating out hundreds of other candidates for a select spot at the Chicago Police Academy.

Graduating with honors, moving up to inspector, to detective, he had felt as if there were no other place on earth where he could make so much of a difference in the world as in the ranks of the Chicago Police Department.

When had it changed?

When had he started to think that he was a soldier in an unwinnable war? When had he started to doubt himself, to doubt his work, to doubt that people had an inner core of good that only needed to be set free from the gritty horror of the streets?

He'd had time, too much time, too many

nights alone, to think about those questions, ever since that moment when he'd been shot. And while he had learned to put off troubling thoughts and questions until the sun settled in for the night, those questions were now invading his days.

Giving up, he grimly slung his pack over his shoulder and marched out.

The afternoon light was dimming in Hubbard Woods. The streets were bustling with wives picking up their husbands at the train station, with shoppers getting last-minute items for their dinners, with children rushing home from school.

There was beauty here. In the golden glint of light, in the dappled leaves that fluttered to the ground, in the potted chrysanthemums—purple and yellow—that decorated the entranceways of shops.

But Logan wasn't thinking of beauty and light. He strode through the streets quickly, heading toward the street that would veer away from downtown, to the small Cape Cod house that was his refuge.

At the corner, his eye was caught by what lay beyond the window at the Sweet Shoppe. He recognized the shock of red hair on the boy who stood in front of the counter, staring with great concentration at the selection of candies.

Impulsively, moving quickly so that he wouldn't come to his senses and stop, Logan entered the store. A ringing bell announced him and prevented him from turning away at the last second.

His eyes met Trish's. She was sitting at one of the tables, drinking a cola with another mother who was happily engrossed in a tall sundae that she was sharing with her son.

He noticed the way Mrs. Eastman's mouth set tightly—no smile—and how her eyes narrowed with concern.

She hadn't gotten her way, so she was pouting, he began to think— *No!* he commanded himself to stop that line of thought.

Just this once, he would give her the benefit of the doubt. He would try, this one time, to see things from her perspective.

It was a habit, a way of looking at the world that had once been an integral part of his nature. And which now required an act of will.

He looked down at Fritz, who gazed at him with a mixture of terror and the sort of steadfast admiration that Logan had seen many times on the faces of boys too young to know better. Kids who didn't know yet that cops in blue uniforms were simply cannon fodder, that part-time karate instructors were just marking time.

"Hello, Fritz," he said. Quickly, before he could change his mind, he asked the counterman for a quarter pound of Gummi Bears candy. He wondered what he would do with that much candy. He didn't like candy, especially not the jellylike stuff he had just asked for.

"Hi, *Sensei*," Fritz mumbled.

Logan felt the boy's pain and winced inwardly. Had he done this? He sensed that Fritz was near to tears. Come to think of it, it had to be pretty humiliating to sit on the sidelines of class. Even though Logan knew that he had had to discipline Fritz or risk the entire class falling apart, his heart now twinged at what Fritz had gone through.

"Hey, you do a good job in class," he said gruffly. "When you pay attention and don't hit anybody, that is."

From across the room, Trish Eastman's stare felt more painful than the burning bullet he had taken four months before.

Logan accepted the paper bag of sticky sweet candy from the counterman and handed over a few bills in return. He crouched down to Fritz's level and held out the bag. The boy, his face a mixture of fear and wonder and surprise, reached in to take a small fistful.

"You have a good kick," Logan continued thoughtfully. "If you work hard at karate, you'll do well. I think you might even be ready for your orange-belt test in January."

"I will?" Fritz said. "An orange belt?"

Logan had to stop himself from smiling with pleasure and delight at the way the boy threw his shoulders back with pride.

"When will I be ready for a black belt?" Fritz pressed, his face earnest and shining with awe.

Logan shook his head and this time he did smile, remembering the years and years of training as he'd worked his way up from a white belt to the coveted black. He'd been sixteen when he had received his first black—and then there were the six levels of black which he had competed for.

If he explained all the time, the focused energy, the daily workouts, the tournaments and the frustration that Fritz had between him and a black belt, Fritz would never come back to class.

With a start of surprise, Logan realized that he saw himself in Fritz. He remembered the impatience he'd had with the repetitive exercises, the determination he'd had to succeed…and suddenly he wanted to communicate to Fritz that soon he would know the freedom of learning to press the limits of his young muscles.

"Let's just focus on an orange belt for now."

"And I can get one in January?"

"Yes, but only if you work hard, pay attention and—" he looked up, and his eyes challenged those of Fritz's mother "—most important, obey the rules."

Fritz looked down, clearly remembering his transgression.

"No fighting," Logan continued in a firm but not unsympathetic voice. "You need to do what I tell you to in class. And what your mother tells you out of class."

Logan was unable to stop himself from looking at her again, but Fritz's mom seemed to have become utterly engrossed in her soda. Maybe too engrossed for her distraction to be natural.

"You're doing well, too, Paul," he said to the other boy who until now had stood by silently staring. The boy's glowing face was a response all its own, and Logan couldn't help checking on Fritz's mother again.

He had conceded, hadn't he? He had given her what she wanted. Yet the sight of Trish East-

man's delicate face in profile, refusing to give
him the slightest credit for his concession, made
him feel a twinge of the same anger he had felt
unconsciously building inside with the passage
of years.

He turned away, quickly saying goodbye to
Fritz and Paul. Walking out, he heard the bells
at the door ring brightly just as Fritz crowed to
his mother, "Did you see that?"

He had given her exactly what she wanted,
exactly what she asked for.

And it made him angry, because the simple
act of praise and encouragement was something
he would have done anyway.

Trish sat on the bleachers sharing a diet cola
with Krysia. The boys sat cross-legged in a row,
waiting for Sensei Powell to arrive with the
other boys. Krysia was discussing needlepoint
patterns with another mother, and since Trish
didn't know anything about the craft, her mind
wandered.

And it wandered, as it had so often in the past
days, to Sensei Logan Powell.

She had to give him credit for turning a bad
situation around so quickly. His words of encouragement in the candy store had been all that

Fritz talked about as they drove home. While she had made dinner for the two of them, Fritz had gone over and over Logan Powell's every word, simultaneously forcing his mother to keep her thoughts on the karate instructor, even when she wanted to firmly put him—and the whole afternoon—behind her.

That night, as Fritz had said his nightly prayers, he had—as always—asked God to bless his mother and himself and his daddy in heaven.

He had also asked God to bless Sensei Logan.

Later, as she'd counted Fritz's friends on her two hands, he had added Logan—bringing the total to eleven.

"Don't you think that's a lot of friends?" Trish asked.

"I've got more friends than even you do," Fritz had answered innocently. And while his words had stung her for just a second, she had realized that he was delighted to be able to believe that.

"I guess you do," she'd said. "I have you and Paul's mother, at least."

"*I'll* always be your best friend," Fritz said earnestly. "And, besides, don't feel bad. You have *Sensei* as a friend, too. That makes three."

Warmed by Fritz's new way of thinking—now *he* was reassuring *her*—she hadn't been able to control her reaction to his last words. It was a good thing Fritz hadn't seen the way his mother's lips had tightened at the mention of the *sensei*.

Logan Powell had done what she had asked, but his kindness was something she hadn't been able to acknowledge in the Sweet Shoppe. That had been unlike her, because she was usually the sort of person who was easy with praise and expressive of gratitude.

But she had been unnaturally silent when Logan had been in the store, and after he left, as Fritz kept talking about him, she'd felt herself withdrawing from the conversation in a defensive way that was unnatural for her.

"Boys!"

The deep, rough-hewn voice announced that class had begun. As he entered the gym, Logan yanked the knot on his black belt, and for an instant, a tantalizing glimpse of his chest caused a collective sigh from the bleachers. Trish couldn't help grinning at these perfectly proper matrons who were so easily swayed by a gorgeous body.

"I wonder if he has any idea what kind of

effect he has on the opposite sex?'' Krysia, sitting at her right, asked.

Trish shook her head. "You know, I hadn't thought of it until this moment, but I bet he doesn't," she said, turning to face her friend.

But as she did, she saw that Krysia's face was glued—with horror—to a point across the gym.

Trish followed her stare. There, in the middle of the gym, was a flash of her son's carrot-topped head, and a confusing tangle of fists and feet and knees. A roar of pain sounded, followed by a shriek of anger. The sensation of mothers all around her leaning forward to observe the fray rushed over her even as her heart sank. *Oh, no, sweetheart. Not again.*

Logan Powell, having entered the gym, sealed Fritz's fate with a single word. "Out!"

"He said I had no daddy!" Fritz declared indignantly.

"Shh!" Trish's voice was a mixture of comfort and protectiveness.

Seated at his desk, staring over the mound of paperwork the Hubbard Woods Park District demanded of its volunteers, Logan hesitated. Momentarily off-balance by Fritz's explanation, he reconsidered his command of not ten minutes before. "No daddy" usually meant only one thing in the small suburb—divorce. Logan was smart enough to know that teasing about such a personal subject was painful—though, of course, it *didn't* justify physical assaults.

But the look on Trish's face hinted at something much more painful than the usual suburban domestic drama. Which meant his usual approach might not be the best option here. Fritz's voice interrupted his thoughts.

"I wanted to kill him," Fritz cried plaintively. "I wanted to beat him into the ground and make him die!"

Trish's eyes opened wide with shock at her son's vehemence. She began to wonder if perhaps she had misjudged Fritz's ability to handle karate, to handle being with other kids, to handle the deep well of emotions that had come out after all this time in such an antisocial outburst. Trish winced as she thought of the other boy's bloodied nose.

"Fritz isn't going back to my class, Mrs. Eastman," Logan said sternly, recognizing immediately that Fritz's anger was dangerous to the rest of the students.

His announcement sparked another explosion of sobs and apologies from Fritz, who had curled up into a ball on top of his mother's lap. She softly caressed the boy's hair, whispered some words to him, and then let him slide to the floor. She watched as Fritz walked out of the coaching office with a child's accusatory stare at his karate instructor.

Ex-karate instructor, Logan reminded himself, trying to ignore the tug at his heart provoked by Fritz's plaintive eyes.

Maybe he should reconsider, take the boy aside, give him another chance....

He sat down behind his desk. Briefly, his karate robe fell open and he reached to pull it into place. Trish looked away quickly. As he closed the folds of fabric over his broad chest, she avoided looking at him by studying the scene outside the window. Children played tag on the Community House playground, an elderly couple fed the pigeons on the lawn, a boisterous group of teens unloaded a truck of props for the fall musical.

"I think you ought to give Fritz one more chance," she said.

Logan was surprised by her voice. With its suggestion of more sass than confidence, it had none of the arrogance that he'd often heard in mothers speaking to him—the ones who considered him a glorified babysitter or an entertainer rented out for their children's delight. Many a Hubbard Woods matron would have just told him flat out that he was going to keep her child in class. Many would tell him that he would do it…or else. A few would threaten his job, as if a volunteer coaching position were his life's work and as if he would tremble at any censure.

"He really likes karate and I think it's important to give him some confidence in his body," Trish continued, clearing her throat. "And he's made friends with Paul, who's also in the class. It's so important for him to make friends. We've just moved here. He needs to have activities that he can share with other kids."

"Maybe he could try not fighting," Logan shot back. As her maternal determination rose, it activated his own defensiveness. "*Not* fighting would win him a lot of friends," he concluded.

She squirmed and Logan had a moment's sense of triumph. He had simply told the truth, and apparently, the truth was too much for her. But that triumph was fleeting, as the victories of all cheap shots are, and left a sour taste in his mouth.

"I'll be honest with you, Sensei Powell. I was

surprised by his feelings being so strong,'' she said. ''I didn't know that he carried around such anger before we signed up for karate—or, at least, I didn't realize how it could be expressed. I think he wants to act out some things.''

''So, how about if he acts out on somebody else's turf?'' Logan asked, driving home his point by leaning forward until his face was close to hers. ''Sign him up for a finger-painting course where he won't do so much damage. I've got a class to run. A few more days with Fritz Eastman in that gym and I might end up with a seriously injured kid.''

She leaned back, surprised by his nearness. Logan caught the clean scent of lilies of the valley. A light, innocent smell that was out of place with the heavy perfumes favored by Hubbard Woods mothers. She was young, he suddenly realized, too young to have already married and divorced.

He looked away, temporarily distracted.

Logan felt no sense of relief about Fritz leaving class. Instead, all he could think of was the child's eyes boring into his at the Sweet Shoppe, with all the admiration and longing and hope that a child has.

''I think you may be too hard on the children,'' Trish said. ''You run your class much too harshly for kids this young, you demand too much perfection and you don't forgive when they misbehave. He's a sweet boy and maybe he's just mimicking your ways when he fights.''

Her barely veiled accusation made him shrug his shoulders. He leaned back in his chair and propped his bare feet—feet which were capable of punching with more force than most men could muster with their fists—on the desk top. At leisure, his masculine body was as daunting as if he were a tiger ready to attack.

''Lady, you think of me as a karate instructor, but I also have a real job,'' he said. ''I'm returning to the police force sometime in the next month or so. I'm on leave because I was shot by a thirteen-year-old who had something to prove to his gang buddies. When I leave here, you're more than welcome to take my place. You can gather up all the kids, get them to talk about their feelings, let them run around all they want, and after six months, what will they know about karate, about discipline, about defending themselves?''

''They don't need to know that stuff—they're five-year-olds!''

Her brown eyes lit up with a brilliant golden

light and her cheeks flushed pink. Momentarily distracted by the sight of her, Logan forced himself to respond.

"Tell that to any kid who's seen violence on the streets," Logan said icily. "It doesn't wait for kids to grow up anymore. If it ever did."

She didn't say anything.

For a moment, he was struck by the forceful flash in her eyes that demanded that he reconsider his words even as she refused to lower herself to speak to him. He wanted the heat and fire of argument, was ready to have her battle him, welcomed the challenge, because—for the barest instant—he thought she might be able to destroy the demons and devils that made him what he was, that made him *not* what he wanted to be. Maybe she had answers he never considered, responses that could force him to change. For that instant, he had thought she could throw him a lifeline, to help him pull himself back into the land of those who know that life is good.

She looked as if she might say something, but then she closed herself off from him. Her eyes seemed to darken. Her shoulders stiffened. She had retreated.

It was then he knew that he hadn't really wanted to win.

"I guess we've discussed this as much as we can," she said with icy calm. "I'll get Fritz out of here."

She stood up and Logan almost told her to sit down, they would work it out, they would give Fritz a second chance.

But her resolve made her unapproachable, made any words dry in his mouth.

She opened the door to the gym and a sudden silence greeted her. The other mothers watched her. The boys were staring at Fritz, who had waited patiently outside.

"Come on," she said quietly to her son.

Logan's heart ached as he watched the dejected boy follow his mother. When Fritz turned once, only once, to shout, "I'm sorry," across the gymnasium, Logan swallowed hard and had to bite his lip very hard to force himself not to call them back.

Chapter Three

"Gosh, Mom, you sure look beautiful," Fritz said.

At her son's compliment, sounding as if it had been pulled from a fifties sitcom, Trish looked up at the mirror. Holding a toothbrush in her mouth and with the faintest trace of turquoise-colored gel on her lips, she didn't regard herself as a glamorous woman.

But to Fritz's eyes, she knew she might look great, if not exactly on the order of a television star. Not even if the television star was the mom from "Leave It To Beaver."

Instead of her daytime uniform of a pocket

T-shirt and black leggings, she wore a charcoal gray jersey dress. Instead of her hair being pulled back in a simple ponytail, she had actually invested ten minutes in blow-drying her hair so that it lay on her shoulders in almost controlled waves.

She had even pulled on a pair of black pumps that had been hiding in her closet and a set of earrings that caused her only the barest twinge of remembrance of her marriage.

She thought it was important to go to the Parent/Child Seminar looking, as nearly as she could, like the other suburban mothers who always managed to look like they belonged wherever they happened to be.

So *beautiful* wasn't what she was striving for—*belonging* was. But she'd still take her son's compliment gratefully.

She finished brushing her teeth and wiped her mouth. Touching her lips with a subtle pink gloss, she was done.

"Thanks, Fritz, that's a nice thing to say. Ready to go?"

He nodded happily.

Trish quelled the butterflies in her stomach and the doubts in her head. Perhaps this was one Parent/Child Seminar they shouldn't attend:

Raising Non-Violent Children in a Violent World.

When she had read the postcard invitation from the school district's Parent-Teacher Board, she'd had an immediate reaction. This was a subject that was vitally important to her and definitely a lecture she should attend. She was excited about going, especially when she saw that the Chicago Police Department would be sending a member of its Gang Crimes Unit.

Then she reconsidered, thinking of the volatile nature of the topic. What if Fritz couldn't handle it? Violence was something that was difficult for any child to understand, much less Fritz.

"The world doesn't wait for children to grow up, if it ever did." She thought of the words that Logan Powell had thrown into her face. If she was honest, she realized that she agreed with him.

It hadn't waited in Fritz's case.

The postcard had stayed tacked onto her kitchen refrigerator with a magnet, alongside dental appointment cards, coupons and favorite snapshots, until Trish had received a call from Libby Joyce, president of the Parent-Teacher Board.

Could Trish please, please, *please* bring a platter of cookies for the reception afterward?

The request had been one of the things which had overcome the niggling doubt that the provocative topic might be too much for Fritz to handle.

"Mom, will we get to stay for the refreshments?" Fritz asked.

Refreshments! Thank heaven he had reminded her.

"Of course we will," Trish said, and she went to the kitchen and pulled the foil-wrapped platter of chocolate brownies she had promised to bring from the refrigerator.

At the school they dropped off the brownies at the cafeteria, where some mothers were already setting up for the refreshment hour. Then she and Fritz went to the auditorium. Seats were filling up rapidly, but Krysia waved to her and so Trish squeezed into the seat next to her and her husband Michael.

Paul and Fritz crawled over the backs of the seats in front of their parents so they could sit near friends. When Fritz left her without even a glance backward, Trish was filled with bittersweet delight—perhaps he was on his way to recovery. He certainly didn't seem any different from any of the other children in the audience.

"You sure you should be here?" Krysia asked as the lights faded.

Trish shook her head, baffled at her friend's question. Although Krysia had become the person to whom she was closest in the suburb, they had never talked about anything other than the usual comparisons of the best place to buy hamburger meat, arrangements for play dates between Paul and Fritz, and the marital problems of the British Royal family.

She'd never opened up, not enough to explain her true fears about Fritz's outbursts in karate class. She had learned that people generally have a very low tolerance for painful true stories—

So how could Krysia know of her inner doubts?

Krysia nodded in the direction of the stage.

Trish looked up and immediately felt a lurch in her stomach. Krysia hadn't been thinking of her doubts. Krysia had been thinking of karate.

"Maybe I shouldn't have come," she said.

"Do you think that Fritz will feel bad?" Krysia asked.

"I don't know," Trish answered truthfully.

Logan Powell stood on the stage. He had

traded his white karate *gi* for a conservative gray suit that he wore with an easy confidence that surprised Trish. While he concentrated on a stack of note cards in front of him on the podium, the principal of Hubbard Woods Elementary held up his microphone and coughed loudly to get people's attention.

Trish closed her eyes, feeling an internal "I told you so" as she remembered her hesitation about coming to this lecture. She sneaked a peek at her son in the row ahead of her. He had noticed Logan Powell, but seemed more concerned about sharing knock-knock jokes with Paul.

Who knew? Maybe Fritz had been able to put the experience of being thrown out of karate behind him.

Trish, on the other hand, couldn't and had dwelled on it more than she would have liked.

She had, at first, felt angry at Logan Powell for throwing her son out of class, holding him responsible for her son crying in the car all the way home, for Fritz making himself so upset that he threw up his dinner, for the night's restless sleep. But long after Fritz seemed to accept Logan's decision, Trish had come to the disturbing and embarrassing conclusion that maybe Logan had been right, and maybe she had more to worry about with Fritz than she had thought.

Oh, he hadn't gotten into any other fights and Trish was thankful for that. But Fritz lacked a confidence that other children possessed, the confidence that things would work out, that their parents were invincible, that they as adults could handle any problem that came up.

But while she might have thought Logan was right that Fritz had a problem, she could still very strongly disagree that booting him out of karate was the solution. After all, the experience had only pointed out once again to Fritz that he was somehow different, somehow defective, when compared to other boys. And that was a terrible lesson to come so quickly to such a young boy. Which had brought her right back, full circle, to the original emotion of anger.

"Welcome, parents, to the first in our series of seminars," the principal said as the audience settled into quiet attention. "We have with us a very special guest—Logan Powell, special investigator on leave from the Chicago Police Department's Gang Crimes Unit. Logan grew up right here in Hubbard Woods. He's spoken to many of the students here tonight in individual classes and he's volunteered to come here tonight to talk to us all about an issue that sometimes feels very removed from us, as Hubbard Woods seems so safe. And yet, we all know that drugs and crime and gangs are starting to get a foothold here—as they have everywhere in America. Logan's going to talk to us tonight about how to protect our children. Let's give Logan a warm welcome...."

The auditorium erupted in applause, which Trish politely joined. As Logan had waited for the principal to finish with his praise and for the audience to quiet its welcome, he had shifted from one foot to the other, and Trish realized it was the first time she had seen any breach in his self-confidence.

But it was only a slight hesitation, unseen by most of the crowd, and in the next instant, he pulled his shoulders back and met the gaze of the audience head-on. As he leaned forward, the spotlight hugged his features and he drew his listeners into his confidence, slipping his note cards into his jacket pocket as if realizing that he could speak as if to a few of his closest friends.

"It's a dangerous world out there," he said, and Trish felt more than heard the audience murmur its agreement. "We want to believe in progress, in the march of civilizing influence, in the good guys winning. But there isn't any progress, we can't civilize our own country and the good guys are very definitely not winning. And the problem is, how do we raise a child to be part of the good-guy team, to *not* become a victim, to *not* become part of the problem.''

''That's so true,'' the woman behind Trish said out loud.

While Logan Powell continued speaking, Trish watched Fritz for some sign of distress, but, like Paul, kneeling on his seat so he could see better, his attention was absolute.

Trish wished she were able to concentrate as well as the boys. She wanted to listen, to absorb Logan's message. Clearly, he had something to say. And yet, she found herself shut off, unable to keep track of his line of thought, her own thoughts as scattered as leaves falling on a windy day.

She knew it was probably a defense mechanism, a way of numbing herself that had gotten her through the last year when her fainter self would have chosen to give up, to pull the covers over her head and never get out of bed.

As if from a distance, she heard the murmurs of approval, the occasional clapping, the ripples of mirth through the audience when Logan broke up the serious message of his talk with wry comments. Logan Powell enthralled his audience, their attention captivated by a man who was so utterly at ease with himself and with his message.

Yet Trish remained apart. After a while, she didn't even listen to his words so much as to his voice, a voice of deep, quiet strength. It was dangerous to listen, because, as he spoke about a war being waged every day on the streets of America, she felt drawn to him, drawn to that quiet strength, drawn to the sense that he could protect.

And she knew, more than anyone should, that there was no safety, no protection in anyone's arms.

Krysia tapped her elbow.

"What's Fritz going to do?" she asked.

Trish was brought instantly to attention. The question-and-answer portion of the program had begun and, in front of her, Fritz's hand was held up, patiently waiting for the signal that he could speak. Trish reached to make him put it down—she didn't want Fritz to draw attention to himself.

Too late.

As she leaned forward, she heard Logan recognize Fritz. The principal walked over to the aisle and leaned over the seats to give Fritz the microphone.

Fritz took it into his hand, and Trish looked up at Logan, hoping vainly to signal him to back off from her son. But Logan's attention was totally focused on her son. Fritz faltered as he breathed into the microphone.

"It's okay," Logan said. "We're listening to you, Fritz. And we want to listen to what you have to say."

Fritz looked up at Logan, seemed reassured, and held the microphone in front of him.

"My name is Fritz Eastman and I'm five years old," he said. He paused and took a deep breath. "My father was murdered last year."

A ripple of disbelief went through the audience. Trish felt tears well up in her eyes. Fritz had never spoken about this before, not to anyone except his mother. He never acknowledged that anything had happened outside of their cocoon.

Trish had prayed, had hoped, had dreamed, of the blessed release of him saying the words, of him sharing the doubts and fears and horror within him. It was an enormous burden for a child to bear. It was also a heavy burden to be the only person he shared it with, in part because she felt so inadequate herself to help him see the best of life.

She had encouraged him, had taken him to a therapist for help, a help that hadn't—in the end—helped very much. She had despaired of him ever breaking free.

But here? To Logan Powell? To an audience of over a hundred people?

"My father was killed by bad guys," Fritz said, and then he stopped, turned around and looked straight into the hushed auditorium. "He went to the grocery store one night after dinner and he was shot by some guys who were robbing the store. They made him lay down next to the clerk and the bad guys shot both of them in the back of the head."

The audience gasped. Fritz looked around, as if he were suddenly confused by the attention his words had received. He hadn't realized the very real power of words, of the images that people had in their minds as he described his father's death. Trish herself closed her eyes, remembering once more that night—waiting and waiting for Robert to come back from a quick errand, knowing when the police officers appeared at her door what they would say before they even said the words.

"Mrs. Eastman, we have terrible news."

She remembered how she had imagined every instant of the robbery, with a vividness that had made her almost believe she had been there. Even now, she sometimes woke up with the sound of a shot at the nightmare's end.

"My God, Trish, I had no idea," Krysia murmured, but Trish didn't reply.

She couldn't.

"Go on, Fritz," Logan encouraged. He stood at the edge of the row of seats, having silently climbed down from the stage while Fritz spoke.

The little boy looked up at Logan.

"My father was killed by bad guys," he repeated, his voice choked with tears. "And sometimes, sometimes, I really wish I could kill them back."

As Logan leaned across the three seats between them, Fritz flung himself into his arms.

Trish stood up, reaching to comfort her son, but she pulled back as she realized that Logan's arm was held out to include her. Stiffly waiting until Fritz broke free of Logan's embrace, she felt the room blur as finally, tears ran down her cheeks.

* * *

"I was wrong about Fritz," Logan said, snatching a brownie as Trish consolidated several platters of cookies into one plate to be left in the teacher's lounge.

During the social hour, as he had made his way across the room toward the buffet table where Trish had been helping with serving coffee, he had been sidetracked half a dozen times. Parents introduced themselves and thanked him for the program. Libby Joyce, from the Parent-Teacher Board, asked if she could pass his name along to the head of the board for another school. The principal wondered if there was a more comprehensive program which he could present to the school.

It wasn't until the gym was thinning out that Logan was his own man again and he wanted very much to talk to Trish. He tugged his red silk tie loose from his collar and bit into a brownie.

"How were you wrong?"

"I didn't realize how much was going on in his life. Maybe I should have given him more of a chance."

She met his gaze, her eyes warily studying him.

"Look, I get the impression that you think I

took advantage of him somehow by letting him talk," Logan said. "You know, I had no idea what he was going to say—"

"I'm glad he talked about it," Trish interrupted. "I've been waiting a long time for him to do that. I'm just a little surprised, that's all."

"Because I'm the guy that hurt his feelings by throwing him out of karate class?"

She nodded.

"I couldn't let him endanger other students."

"Sometimes I remember that," she admitted.

"But I might have been wrong to throw him out, and maybe I was wrong about you, too," he continued. "I thought you were someone sheltered, someone who didn't understand the real world. I tend to think that about people who live outside the city. I owe you an apology."

He popped the rest of the brownie in his mouth before he could say anything more. At the rate he was going, he would start apologizing for everything he had ever done wrong since he was a toddler!

But something about the pretty young widow made him feel like he could do it…and she wouldn't laugh or take advantage of his feelings.

"Apology accepted," she said graciously.

"But maybe I should start with a thank-you. You got him to open up tonight."

She nodded in the direction of the children who were playing on the opposite side of the gym. Although not in the center of the group, Fritz was nonetheless a part of things, running and shrieking with Paul as an older child chased them.

"Doesn't he look lighter already?" Trish asked. "As if the weight has lifted from his shoulders?"

They watched Fritz and Paul run to the refreshments table, each snatching a cookie before the last platter was covered with Saran Wrap.

Trish sighed inwardly, her heart filled with love for her son. She knew the healing wasn't over, not by a long shot. Fritz might never completely recover from the shock of his father's murder. But something had started, something like the first tentative buds of spring that swell to blossoming renewal.

"I thought we could start over," Logan said, startling Trish from her thoughts. "With karate. I think it could be good for him. I know it sounds like karate teaches kids to fight each other and chop bricks in half with their bare hands, but it doesn't. Karate teaches anyone, especially kids, how to have the confidence *not* to fight. That might be good for Fritz.''

''I hope you're right,'' Trish said.

The principal turned the lights on and off twice as a warning to parents that the evening was over. Several mothers called their children, preparing to leave.

''Could I buy you a cup of coffee?'' Logan asked.

Trish's heart pounded and her eyes met his. She sensed an ambiguity in his invitation. On the one hand, it seemed directly related to talking about Fritz—a simple enough matter. But his tone of voice also had the suspicious softness of a more social invitation—one she couldn't accept.

She wasn't a girl anymore. She had grown up. She had married. And she had been widowed.

Would she have married Robert if she'd known how quickly tragedy could strike? She suspected she would have, if only to have the boy she loved so much. And yet, could she ever again make a choice that would lead to so much hurt, for herself and her son?

This was a man who put his life on the line every day and seemed to revel in the proximity to danger, Trish had known that from the first.

So no matter how attractive, or how the sincere appeal in his green eyes made her want to agree to anything he said, she knew she had to turn down his invitation. He could never be a part of their lives, except in the most peripheral of ways.

The memory of her son, standing by her husband's casket, his tears like a river of grief on his cheeks, was enough to squelch any misgivings about her decision. She would never expose her son to that again.

"I'm asking because I want to talk more about Fritz," Logan added. "They're about to throw us out of the gym."

He was right. Krysia had won the struggle to get Paul into a jacket and was waving a cheery goodbye from the door.

Two janitors flipped the empty table on its side and folded its legs. Fritz stood at the water fountain.

The gym had cleared out.

Trish relaxed, and allowed herself a smile at her own foolishness. It was a relief to discover that his invitation hadn't the slightest personal or romantic edge to it. He *had* really wanted to talk about Fritz, and Trish trusted him on this. He had helped her son, and if he thought he could help more, as a good mother, she would listen.

"I haven't got a baby-sitter," Trish said. "Another time?"

"How about meeting me for a cup of coffee at the Espresso Café around ten tomorrow morning?" Logan asked, trying to keep his voice casual. He'd thought she would give him the brush-off for sure. Taking in her softened hair and breathing in the lily of the valley scent that he was becoming dangerously familiar with, he hadn't dared hope she would agree to meet with him—to talk about Fritz, of course, he reminded himself. But she had. Ignoring the unexpected rush of warmth this gave him, he waited for her response.

"Fine," Trish said, just as Fritz crashed into her to put his arms around her. "Fritz, say goodnight to Mr. Powell."

"Good night, *Sensei*," Fritz said.

Trish felt a tug in her heart as she watched her son's gaze follow Logan as the older man crossed the gym, picked up his backpack and trench coat from the bleachers' rise, and waved from the doorway.

Chapter Four

After dropping off Fritz at kindergarten, Trish found a parking place in front of the Café Espresso. She checked the rearview mirror for traces of a coffee mustache, kicked in the emergency brake of her Jeep, and grabbed a handful of change for the parking meter.

When she worked at home, as a freelance bookkeeper for several Hubbard Woods businesses, she did it on the run, on the dining room table, in her pajamas or her mom uniform of T-shirts and leggings. Her business was just starting, a supplement to the life insurance money that kept the bills paid. Trish hoped that

by the time she used up the insurance money,
her business would be profitable enough to support her and Fritz.

Maybe she'd have an office. Maybe she'd be
able to afford a housekeeper, so she could work
straight through the day instead of grabbing an
hour here and there, squeezed into the gaps in
Fritz's schedule. And maybe she could afford
more than one suit.

In deference to her meeting with Logan, she
now wore that navy blue suit—the one she
pulled out of the closet when she met with clients for the first time, the one she wore when a
client wanted her to confer with their account-
ants. For reasons she couldn't, or wouldn't, fully
explain to herself, she felt that the clothes kept
her sensibilities firmly on track. On a business
track.

For this meeting was like business, very much
like the meetings she had had with therapists and
psychiatrists and experts who had promised to
help Fritz.

Nothing had worked, so she had moved to a
safe suburb, or at least a suburb that was quieter
by far than the city, where the late-night rush of
sirens was a constant reminder to Fritz of catastrophe. She had moved and was trying to give

him a life as normal as possible. Logan might be able to help her with this.

Last night, for the first night she could remember in a long time, Fritz had slept without nightmares, without waking her with his sobs.

That fact alone had convinced her that Logan Powell might be the key to her son's recovery.

Logan sat at a booth by the window overlooking the ravine where the commuter trains passed, his attention taken up with a sheaf of papers in front of him. But as the bell over the café's door cheerily announced Trish's entrance, he stuffed the papers into a manila folder. He stood as she approached him, and she was surprised he was also wearing a suit, a lighter gray version of the one he had worn to the seminar the evening before.

"I have a meeting with the school superintendent in an hour," he explained, sensing her puzzlement. "It's probably better to not wear jeans."

She smiled, unexpectedly, charmed by the sparkle in his eyes. Squelching her sudden urge to touch him, she sat down across from him and asked, "What's your meeting about?"

He signaled the waitress.

"The school district wants me to develop a

full-time program for teaching drug and crime awareness, and I might be able to help them out—at least, until I go back to the police department. Do you want a cup of coffee?''

"Thanks, I'd love one," Trish said. "How would you fit this into your schedule?" she asked Logan as the waitress dropped a menu on the table, poured coffee into the cup at Trish's setting, and then left.

"I'm not sure," Logan admitted. "For somebody who's on a leave of absence, I do seem to have a busy schedule.''

They laughed together, and Trish took a sip of the rich, cinnamony coffee. His eyes lingered on her, startling her. She thought for an instant that something was wrong, and she reflexively brushed her mouth with her napkin. Then, she realized what she was seeing.

Attraction.

Just the barest, subtlest moment of attraction. She was certain that Logan was just noticing her, just for an instant communicating normal, everyday masculine appraisal.

No, no, *no,* she thought to herself, ending that thought. She had been able to dismiss attraction to Logan Powell in an instant when she first saw him in the Community House gymnasium, in the heat and fire of anger at him, and though the anger was gone, those brief feelings had to be put in proper perspective.

He was, as Krysia had pointed out, an unbearably handsome man. But like Krysia's attraction, Trish's feelings were purely theoretical, something that could be joked about between girlfriends but never acted upon.

Maybe his feelings were theoretical, too, she thought. And maybe his appraising look was nothing more than a reflex that could be provoked by any woman. Trish ignored the flash of dismay that thought engendered. What was wrong with her?

"You wanted to talk about Fritz," Trish said abruptly.

He registered brief surprise at her awkward change of conversation, but he obligingly pulled out a black date book from his briefcase.

"I think that if he has some extra help, some one-on-one tutoring, he can get back into class in a month," Logan said. "So, if you agree to it, I'd like to set up a schedule of individual training."

"You want to tutor Fritz on your own?" Trish asked.

"I think it will make all the difference in the

world," Logan said. "A few weeks of individual work and then he can rejoin the class. That's what you wanted, isn't it?"

Trish stopped herself as she heard the barest hint of defensiveness in his voice. He was thinking she was rude, and yet, she was simply shocked.

"I don't know what to say."

She wanted to say thank-you, she wanted to say yes, but the cost of the group karate lessons had been more than a week's worth of groceries—how much more he must charge for individual tutoring!

"How about Tuesday and Thursday evenings at five at the Community House gym," Logan offered, leafing through the pages of his date book.

"Wait!" Trish exclaimed. "How much do you charge for individual lessons?"

"The same that I charge the Community House administration for my services," Logan said with a mischievous smile. "Nothing."

"But you have so much packed into your schedule," Trish persisted.

"I want to do this," Logan said firmly. "I look at Fritz and see just a little corner of the world that I can make a difference in."

The words did nothing to allay her concerns.

"Look, I don't want to appear ungrateful, I just need to make sure that there's no, um..."

"No hidden price?"

She nodded.

"Well, there is one," he said.

She caught her breath.

"I was hoping you could invite me to dinner one night after class," Logan said. "I only moved back to Hubbard Woods when my leave started and I have to tell you that I'm pretty isolated...."

He left out the fact that while he had been very successful at filling up nearly every minute of his days, his nights remained empty. And that emptiness had pressed against him, taunting him with the suggestion that his life had lost its meaning. It was even harder to live in the house he had grown up in, the house where he and his brother had grown and played and fought. Even the streets came alive with memories at night, so late-night walks to burn off pent-up frustrations didn't work.

Any excuse to get out was worth taking, although the few times that he had driven outside of the small suburb to a bar or a restaurant had left him cold. A friend, one that didn't come with the baggage of lifelong memories, was what he needed.

And if she was attractive as well, it didn't hurt. Or so he told himself.

She hesitated, and Logan had a sudden realization.

She's worried I'm hitting on her, he thought.

She obviously had no interest in any kind of intimate relationship. He wasn't in her league, she wasn't ready, whatever the reason, it didn't matter. He didn't have any intention of getting involved with someone from Hubbard Woods, anyway—in a few short weeks, he'd probably be back in his spare Chicago apartment, working late-night shifts and he wouldn't want any encumbrances.

"This isn't a pick up, if that's what you're worried about," he explained. "I'm talking about a simple meal between friends. I feel like such a fifth wheel out here in the suburbs, and I thought you might feel the same way."

She looked at him warily, uncertain if she felt better because he was making it so clear that he didn't have the slightest bit of interest in her.

Or if she felt worse.

Sometimes, in the past year, she had felt so much older than twenty-seven. As if she had passed through her twenties and thirties and forties and was too old for carefree flirtation, dating, romance.

Of course, to be fair, there were plenty of women who were many years her elder who had all the energy for interacting with the other half of the human race.

But Logan's hasty determination to place this invitation clearly on the footing of casual friendship just confirmed her opinion of herself as too old, too dowdy, too tired, too…something for lighthearted romance.

She shook the small hurt off easily.

"All right," she said. "Dinner."

"How about Tuesday night?" Logan said. "If you can drop him off at the Community House around five o'clock, when my last class ends, I'll drive him back home for dinner around six."

"Dinner on Tuesday. I'll have Fritz at the gym by five," she promised.

The rules of friendship agreed upon, they finished up their coffee. Logan paid the check and, after they shook hands goodbye on the sidewalk, Trish felt the nearly uncontrollable urge to count.

After all, she had gained something very important in that restaurant.

"I guess you're right, Fritz," she whispered to herself as she watched Logan stride purposefully away in the direction of the school-district headquarters. "I have three friends in Hubbard Woods—Krysia, you, and now Logan."

"Mom, we're home!"

The back screen door squealed as it was opened and then slammed shut.

Trish looked up from the salad she was tossing to see Fritz bounding into the kitchen, his face flushed and happy. Behind him, filling the doorway, stood Logan.

Just as their eyes met, she turned away.

The familiar words tugged at her heart. They were words that had been repeated a hundred times in her marriage.

We're home.

Words she had once taken for granted, not recognizing how precious they were. Trish felt herself stop, midthought, and knew that it was a signal that she had invested so much into insuring Fritz's recovery that she had missed the signs of her own heartache at the loss of her husband.

She had mourned for Fritz but not for herself.

But Trish willed herself not to succumb to

reminiscence. She reminded herself that things change. And one of those changes, the good kind, was very evident on Fritz's happy face.

"Did you have a good time?" she asked, knowing in advance the answer.

"Oh, yeah!" Fritz exclaimed. "I'm learning the eight-step *kata*. I know I can get that orange belt by January!"

Trish looked up at Logan.

"Eight-step what?"

He shrugged. "It's a karate exercise," he explained, accepting her gesture toward a stool beside the counter as an invitation to sit down.

As he passed Trish, the subtle smell of his body—citrus mixed with musk—told her that he had been working hard. And adding Fritz to his schedule must have made it even harder.

And it certainly deserves the best meal I can put together, Trish thought, wondering briefly if the plump hamburgers, tossed salad and baked potatoes were special enough for the occasion. She reached into the lowest drawer of the counter and pulled out a faded blue linen tablecloth and matching napkins.

"He has to learn all eight steps and a series of punches before he can test for the belt," Logan explained. "I thought if I worked on it with him a few weeks before putting him back in the class, he'll be confident enough to keep cool when he feels cornered. And to get an orange belt will be a big boost.''

"Does he have to fight anybody in the test?'' Trish asked.

Logan shook his head and accepted a glass of white wine from her.

"Not until he tests for a brown belt, which won't happen until his teens.''

"Well, that makes me feel great. Let's toast Fritz's orange belt,'' Trish said, raising her diet cola can to tap her son's juice glass.

"And my teacher,'' Fritz said.

Trish nodded.

"To Sensei Logan,'' she added.

Logan and Fritz set the table while she put the final touches on dinner. When Logan held a chair for her, she accepted with what she hoped passed for gracious-hostess manners. Seeing the interplay between the two adults, Fritz froze, his fork halfway to his mouth, and then he remembered his manners.

"Sorry, Mom,'' he said, and put his fork down. He grabbed his napkin from beside his plate and shoved it onto his lap.

Trish sat down, and smiled forgiveness at her

son. It had been so long since she had expected good table manners. When it was just the two of them, it didn't really matter.

As soon as Fritz and Logan began eating, Trish relaxed, knowing that the simple yet hearty fare was exactly right. Ordinarily, Fritz was a picky eater. Often, caught up in his own thoughts at the dinner table, his appetite disappeared. This evening, he polished off one hamburger with gusto and, to Trish's delight, reached for a second one.

"I worked out real hard," he explained.

"He sure did," Logan seconded.

Fritz prattled on as they ate, explaining every detail of his school, his friends and his classes to Logan. Although Trish thought of herself as close to her son, she was surprised at all the new information she learned.

After the three of them thought they couldn't eat another thing, she brought out a bubbling peach cobbler and ice cream.

"Can I take mine into the living room and watch Nickelodeon?" Fritz begged.

"Sure," Trish said, noting that his eyes were starting to droop. He needed some time to relax and television, just a little of it, might be the best thing for him.

She carried his plate and fork to the living room and he followed with his milk glass. "Not too loud," she cautioned as she left him sitting on the couch.

When she came back to the dining room, she found Logan stacking plates. "Just leave all this stuff," she said. "Want some coffee?"

"Coffee would be great."

Picking up the plates and silverware, he followed her into the kitchen and she put on a pot of coffee.

"I guess I was pretty forward to invite myself over here," Logan said, as she set the pot on the stove. "It was a great dinner, first thing I've eaten in weeks that wasn't pulled out of a freezer and thrown in a microwave. But I might have made a mistake inviting myself over here."

Trish felt a hot blush on her face, wondering if she had said or done anything to make him feel that he was unwelcome. She had wanted to be a good hostess, to show her appreciation for his volunteering to teach Fritz, and she had genuinely begun to feel that Logan Powell might turn into a real friend—at least a friend for her son, and maybe even for herself.

"We've loved having you over," she said. "What was the mistake in that?"

"I saw how you looked at me when I first walked into the apartment," he said.

Trish felt tears welling up in her eyes.

"What did I do wrong?" Logan asked softly.

"You didn't do anything wrong," she explained. "When Fritz came into the house, he was bursting with excitement—the same kind of happiness and energy that he had before my husband was shot. When I saw you standing in the doorway…"

"It cut a little close?" he prompted.

"Yeah, it did. I felt like I had been thrown back in time, back to when we lived in Chicago, in a supposedly safe neighborhood, and Robert would come home with Fritz from shopping or a walk or a trip to the ice-cream shop on the corner. And Fritz would have this way of leaping into a room, with all the remarkable energy that boys have, shouting 'Hello' and 'We're home'…"

"Just like tonight," Logan said.

"Yeah, just like tonight," Trish agreed.

She turned away, studying the view outside the window, the quiet street along the pharmacy's entrance.

"I looked up from the salad when he came

in,'' she continued. ''And, for just the briefest instant, I was...''

''Disappointed that it was me,'' Logan said.

''No!'' She cried out. ''Well, maybe I was, a little. Mostly, I was just thrown back in time for a moment. Reminded of things long ago.''

''So it wasn't disappointment on your face?'' Logan asked, leaning on the countertop next to her. ''Not disappointment?''

Trish shook her head.

''I didn't mean to make you feel... unwelcome,'' she said.

He reached and brushed a tear that had fallen, unbeckoned, to her cheek.

He cupped her face in his hand. She felt the catch in her throat as she tried to speak.

She should turn away, before her vulnerabilities got her into trouble. She knew, with clarity, that he could easily take advantage of her, could exploit her with just a kiss.

She felt the danger as he pulled her to him. But there was no kiss. There was no hint of seduction. Instead, he pulled her into his arms for a hug.

It was safe. It was comforting. It was chaste.

Even so, Trish found herself opening up to urges she didn't want. The attraction she had felt for him interfered with her ability to keep within herself all the emotions so tightly controlled for so long. She felt dizzy, frightened that she would somehow make a fool of herself—would cling too tightly to his arms, would open herself too much to the gnawing sense of need within.

So while she opened her arms one moment, at the next she felt a chill as she pulled away.

"Logan, please don't," she said, with more primness than she liked in her voice.

He backed off immediately, straightening up.

"I'm sorry," he said. "I didn't mean..."

"Don't worry—I didn't think you meant anything other than friendship," she said quickly. "I'm not ready for any of this, not even the innocent hugs."

"Everybody needs a friend."

"Yes, I need a friend, but I can't handle anything more. I'm not saying that you're offering anything more," she added hastily, her cheeks hot once again.

If she was totally honest, she would say that it was her own reaction to him that she couldn't handle.

"You can't handle my hugging you, even if it's perfectly innocent?"

She hesitated. She had never really thought it

through before, but she knew now that even the most innocuous touch could open up within her certain vulnerabilities that were better left closed.

Even if he was interested in her, even if he was as tempted as she was, she couldn't let herself open up.

Especially to him. He was a cop, a man who made his living putting himself in the line of fire. His world was one where there was no safety, no refuge. And there was Fritz to consider, as well as her own fragile heart.

"I guess that's my answer," Logan said softly.

"I'm sorry."

"Don't be sorry," he said. "It clarifies things for me. Friends are more important than lovers, anyway. Lovers come and go—but a friend can be a friend forever. Although friends have to make up the rules to their relationship as they go along, just as lovers do."

She wasn't sure she agreed with that, and she wondered about the experiences that had made that statement a part of his life. But she nodded, relieved to agree with him, relieved to know that an important issue in their relationship had been settled.

Even as she thought this, she felt a tug of regret. He was, after all, a handsome man with a broad-shouldered body that could make a woman feel every inch a woman. And the feelings she had experienced in his arms, however frightening, had been thrilling.

But she wasn't a teenager anymore, able to follow whatever whim she chose. The stakes were too high. There was somebody who depended on her to be strong, to keep it together. Just as she had for the past year, never letting herself give in to the darkness, always keeping a no-nonsense perspective for Fritz's sake.

"Listen, I gotta be going," Logan said.

"What about the coffee?" she asked politely. Switching off the stove when he didn't answer, she followed him to the living room.

He paused in the doorway and she came to stand behind him.

Fritz, sporting a milk and peach cobbler mustache, lay sleeping on the couch, arms cradling his empty dessert plate. A commercial loudly trumpeting the virtues of a new breakfast cereal couldn't drown out his delicate snoring.

"Tell the little tiger I'll see him Thursday," Logan said.

"You still want to...?"

"Of course," he said. "Lady, you know how to make a great hamburger and an even better cobbler, but you don't know anything about how a man operates. I keep my promises—when I say I'll do something, I'll do it. I want that boy of yours in the gym at five on Thursday."

Chapter Five

Three weeks is a long time, Trish thought to herself as she watched her son punch, block and parry with an invisible enemy. The only sound in the empty gym was the *swooosh* of his *gi* as he did the graceful exercise and the distant *thump! thump!* of the aerobics class in the studio upstairs. It was like watching the perfection of a ballet and Trish was genuinely impressed that the little boy who couldn't manage a jumping jack without collapsing into paroxysms of laughter three weeks before was now performing with such concentration and determination.

"What do you think?"

"I think he's great," Trish said, shaking her head in amazement. "But, then, I don't know anything about karate."

"Trust me. He is great. He's very smart and, once he settles down, he pays attention and works very hard. If he sticks with it, he can be a black belt. Although not soon enough for him," Logan added, remembering his own impatience with himself as a child.

"Thank you for the time you've spent with him. We're both grateful."

He shrugged off her thanks with a flushed nod and shouted across the gym.

"Fritz, let's show your mom one more time! Start from the beginning."

Her boy came to a halt, bowed once to Logan and Trish, and began again the intricate series of moves.

"Is he ready to go back into the regular class?"

Logan nodded.

"On Tuesday, bring him to the four-fifteen class," he said. "I'd like him to show you the eight-step *kata* and the *Hans Shodun* kicks a few more times and then I've got to get out of here. I'm running a little behind."

"Hot date?" Trish teased, feeling her mouth

go dry. They had worked very hard in the past weeks to replicate the lighthearted banter of just plain friends.

Could a man and a woman be just friends?

Or, to put the question the way that Trish had to think of it, could *she* be just friends with a man as attractive as Logan, a man who could make tingling feelings break out all over even the strongest woman?

Logan, she figured, would answer the question with a hearty "Sure, why not?"

He seemed able to joke around and he hadn't reached out to touch her once since the first night in her apartment. He was a perfect buddy, a great pal, a wonderful friend.

Trish, however, hadn't quite gotten the hang of it yet and her answer would have to be given with a great deal more hesitation.

"Some hot date!" Logan pretended to complain. "Three hundred parents at the Kenilworth School. I'm doing the same program I did at Fritz's school."

Trish exhaled. She hadn't even noticed she'd been holding her breath.

If Logan had a girlfriend, it would make their relationship better, wouldn't it? It would put to rest—definitively—the silly daydreams she occasionally had and the funny fluttering feeling she had when he was around. Maybe the girlfriend would become a friend to Trish, as well, become someone to enlarge Trish's own social circle. At least, that was how Trish tried to look at it, working to persuade herself that a foursome of Fritz, Logan, Trish and another woman—a more beautiful, smarter and livelier woman, no doubt—would make for a lot of fun.

There were all kinds of other reasons that he should go out, have hot dates, get involved with a woman—but Trish couldn't think of these reasons right then.

Three hundred parents in Kenilworth sounded a lot safer.

"That's too bad," she said. "I was going to invite you to dinner at the new Mexican restaurant across from our apartment. To celebrate Fritz's progress and to thank you for all you've done."

The invitation, which would have been too forward three weeks ago, was now natural after all of Logan's work carefully nurturing Fritz's skills in karate.

There had been two other such dinners, spur-of-the-moment-type meals of homemade soup and sandwiches that Trish had stretched to include Logan when she'd had to ask him to drive Fritz home from lessons because clients needed last-minute work finished. Both times, Trish had hastily put candles on the table and brought out the linen napkins in order to give the dinners a festive atmosphere which overcame, in her mind, the ordinariness of her food.

And last Saturday morning, when Trish had taken Fritz out for errands, they had run into Logan at the McDonald's. They'd spent the rest of the morning walking the commercial streets of Hubbard Woods together until Fritz had persuaded the two adults that he had better get a chance to play in the park or there would be a rebellion. Logan had even stayed with Fritz at the park long enough to let Trish do some grocery shopping. And when he had helped carry the bags home, it had felt like the most natural thing in the world to ask him to stay for dinner. What else could she do with a man who was willing to play a game of Candy Land with her son while she cooked?

Though she appreciated the casual friendship that Logan offered, Trish still found herself a little off-balance by things as simple as the way the wind lifted the curls of his hair when he pushed Fritz on the swing or the sparkle of his eyes in the soft candlelight. Even the satisfying way that he first resisted the offer of seconds and then succumbed to her homemade desserts affected her, reminding her that her feelings for him were growing in ways that she couldn't have predicted and couldn't seem to control.

And always in the back of her mind was the remembrance that he would return to the police force, that his job at the Community House would be taken over by someone else when he returned to the beat.

"You're talking about having dinner at Felicia's?" Logan asked.

She nodded.

"You've been so wonderful to tutor him," she said. "I know that volunteering twice a week is no small thing with a schedule as hectic as yours. It's made such a difference to Fritz."

"Oh, yeah, he's getting good," Logan acknowledged, nodding sheepishly as Fritz continued his moves on the mat.

"You've also helped in other ways," Trish said, wishing that he weren't so embarrassed by praise and thanks. "Fritz is sleeping better, he's less pouty and his teachers say he's not overreacting to teasing the way he used to."

"So, what's my reward?" Logan teased, suggestively winking.

"Dinner," Trish said. "How about tomorrow night, are you free?"

She ignored a nudging within her that made her wonder if she had other plans besides dinner for Fritz.

Trish Eastman? Other plans?

Forget it, she thought, my evenings are free between now and Fritz's graduation from high school.

"Hmm," Logan mused. "Friday night? Hubbard Woods's most eligible bachelor? I can meet you there around eight."

Trish shook her head.

"Six," she corrected. "Fritz can't stay up that late."

He laughed and agreed to six.

If he was disappointed that dinner would be a threesome, it didn't show as he walked toward Fritz. And, for that, Trish was pleased. Nothing could be worse than for them to have a tug of war over their friendship.

As Fritz finished his last precise movements, Logan tousled his hair and Trish noted the look of adoration that Fritz gave to his karate instructor.

"You're back in the class, Fritz," Logan announced.

"I am? *Awesome!*"

"You've done a lot of work and it shows," Logan said. "Now, I've got to get going."

Fritz's face fell.

"You're not coming to dinner tonight? Mom said we could go to the Mexican restaurant. Paul went there with his parents last night and they got to take home the paper fans that came with their drinks."

"We're going tomorrow night," Trish explained. "Logan's busy tonight. You can get a paper fan tomorrow."

"Okay," Fritz said, only mildly disappointed.

"I gotta run," Logan said. "Six o'clock, right?"

Trish nodded.

He gave a quick high five to Fritz and headed for the locker room.

As Trish led Fritz to the parking lot, he explained to her all the moves of the *kata* and demonstrated several kicks and punches. And, after he had explained karate to her, he switched to telling her all about the doings at his kindergarten. Trish breathed in the cool, moist evening air and uttered a quick prayer of thanks.

He was happy.

Her boy was happy.

"Mom, we can't have dinner with *Sensei* tomorrow," Fritz said after he finished his nightly prayers.

"Why not?"

"I just remembered," he said mournfully. "You promised me that I could go to Paul's house for the pajama party."

Trish groaned.

Of course. The pajama party. It wasn't Trish who had any plans. It was Fritz.

Paul's older sister was having a sleep over at the Miller house and—to give Paul a treat—Krysia had invited Fritz to have dinner and watch a few kids' videos with Paul. He was also invited to sleep over if his courage held up—although Krysia had warned that her daughter's first sleep over had ended with a two a.m. phone call asking for a ride home. Since the Millers lived in the next block, Trish and Krysia thought it wouldn't be a problem to give it a try. And the boys were so excited by the idea that it was hard to deny them the opportunity.

"Okay, I'll call Logan tomorrow and tell him

that we can have dinner another night,'' Trish said.

After she dropped off Fritz at the Millers, Trish walked back to Felicia's, which was just across the street from her own apartment. She had left several messages on Logan's machine, but when she didn't get any return call from him, she worried he might not have even checked his machine and he might believe she was being rude and standing him up.

So she had decided to wait a few minutes for him, just to make sure that he wasn't inconvenienced by waiting.

She stood near the doorway, making way when families and the occasional couple arrived. Even at the early hour, or maybe especially at the early hour, the restaurant was filling up quickly.

Good thing, Trish thought, knowing that if there was a long wait for a table, she couldn't be pressured by Logan, or her stomach, into staying. Although both Paul and Fritz had been thrilled at the idea of a slumber party—complete with videos, popcorn, a late bedtime and a trip to the pancake house in the morning—Trish had made it clear that she would be home all night in case Fritz couldn't handle being away from her.

"Go ahead and have dinner with Logan," Krysia clucked now as she shooed Trish from the door. "The boys will have a great time and even if Fritz panics, that won't happen for hours. You deserve some time out for yourself and I'm glad we can help out in return."

That last was a reminder of the two times that Trish had taken Paul for dinner and a movie in order to let the Millers go out for an evening. Trish had thought of these favors as treats for herself and Fritz, who had stopped complaining of having no friends.

"Don't worry, I'm going to have a blast on my own. I've got a great movie to watch and a pint of jamocha fudge ice cream," Trish said, mentally adding the invoices and checks from the local bakery that needed to be reconciled. "What more could a girl ask for?" she added.

Krysia shook her head.

"Who knows what might develop between you two."

"Nothing," Trish said firmly. "Absolutely nothing."

"Why? He's a nice guy, more handsome than a man has a right to be, and he's interested from what I can figure. He's a catch,'' Krysia said, leaning back from the front doorjamb into her living room to shout at the assembled teenaged girls that they had better turn down that stereo…or else.

"I'm not interested,'' Trish said.

"Show me any red-blooded, normal American woman who wouldn't be interested in him,'' she said with mock disbelief.

"Well, anyhow, I'll be at home,'' Trish said.

She shouted a goodbye to Fritz, who was jumping up and down on the sofa with Paul in time to the latest bit by a teen hearthrob. Eight teenaged girls danced around the living room floor, while another three huddled around the telephone.

"Have a great time,'' she said wryly.

"I'd rather have dinner with Logan Powell,'' Krysia mused. "You're crazy to not grab at all life has to offer you, Trish.''

Trish didn't stay to contradict her.

At six-fifteen, people were beginning to mill about the small hallway leading into the restaurant, holding brightly colored drinks as they waited for a free table.

Logan must have gotten my message, Trish thought, deciding it was safe to leave.

As she walked across the street to her apartment, she felt an unexpected disappointment. An evening alone with the accounts of Hubbard Woods Bakery, a video, ice cream and a pile of laundry didn't seem quite as exciting as it had scant hours before.

"Hey, wait!"

She whirled around to see Logan, dressed in a black warm-up suit, striding purposefully across the street.

"What did you do?" he exclaimed. "Give up on me already? Sorry I'm late. It's been an unbelievable day. I've been a half hour late for everything."

"Half hour late for everything except dinner," Trish pointed out. "It's only six-fifteen."

"Yeah, but that's because I really wanted to be here," he said with an enthusiasm that made Trish instantly feel guilty about canceling. "Come on, let's head across the street. The place is mobbed. By the way, where's Fritz?"

As he reached for her hand, she pulled away.

"Fritz is at a sleep over. I'm sorry, I left a couple of messages on your machine. I thought you would get them, but it sounds like you didn't have a chance to call in."

"No, I didn't," he said, his voice dropping its usual cheer. "So, what are you saying? You don't want to have dinner if it's just me and not my little sidekick?"

"I was thinking we could do this another time," she said.

"What are you doing tonight?"

"I've got some work I have to do, and then there's some laundry…"

"Have dinner with me now."

Trish looked at the crowd milling about the sidewalk in front of the restaurant.

"The place is mobbed, it'll take an hour to get in."

"So?"

She shook her head.

"I don't think so. I promised Krysia I'd be at home, just in case Fritz needs to bail out. It's his first sleep over."

"First one? God, I remember my first sleep over at Joey Grodzicki's house when I was five. My parents had to come pick me up at eleven o'clock because I suddenly decided I couldn't sleep without my blanket."

Trish laughed. "So you understand."

"Yeah, I guess I do," he said. "So, you're going to eat a TV dinner at home, watch part of a video, do some laundry, wonder to yourself whether socks are part of a conspiracy to disappear in the dryer, and then eat ice cream straight out of the container? Pecan crunch?"

Trish shook her head. "Jamocha fudge."

"I knew it! I just got the flavors wrong."

"Just a good guess."

"No, it's simple deduction."

"Oh, really?"

"Yeah, that's what I do every Friday night. Laundry, microwave dinners, videos."

They laughed together, and Trish softened as she realized that maybe, just maybe, he had been looking forward to this dinner. It was unfair of her to tie up his plans for Friday night and then to cancel at the last minute.

The margin of guilt was all Logan needed to press his advantage.

"How about if we order out from Felicia's?" Logan asked. "That way you can hear the phone if it rings, we can both have something slightly more civilized than frozen food, and you can still kick me out by nine o'clock. After all, I have laundry to do, too."

With just the slightest boyish smile, he was doing his best to overcome her qualms.

And it was working.

"We have only one very important question to settle in this relationship," he said solemnly.

"What's that?"

"Whether to order two sides of guacamole."

Chapter Six

"Two burrito grandes, two orders of guaca-mole with chips, a side of Spanish rice, and, to top it all off—" Logan pulled a final foam container from the bag with a flourish "—a dessert of tortillas dipped in cinnamon sugar."

"It sounds, it looks, it smells wonderful," Trish said, admiring the dinner that crowded her kitchen counter.

"So let's dig in," Logan said, producing a set of plastic cutlery from a second smaller paper bag.

"I've already set the dining room table," Trish said. "You sit down and relax, I'll put this on plates."

"Plates?" Logan asked, snatching a chip. *"Plates? Real* forks? *Cloth* napkins. You're way too civilized."

"Maybe it comes from so many years of being a wife," Trish said easily, surprised that the joking admission didn't cause any twinges of pain. She pulled two plates from the overhead cabinet and began the task of apportioning the delectable food. "Do you want to grab the serving bowl from on top of the refrigerator to put the chips in?"

"That reminds me, I've never really known much about your marriage. How long were you a wife?" Logan asked as he followed her instructions to put rice and guacamole into serving bowls.

"Five years, nearly six. I dropped out of Northern Illinois University to marry Robert. He was two years older than I and had gotten a job as an electrical engineer here in Chicago, so I just followed him."

"And then you had Fritz," Logan added.

Trish pulled a large serving tray, a holdover wedding present from so many years before, from behind the sink. She placed the plates on the tray and handed it to Logan.

"We had Fritz very quickly," she agreed, taking the bowl of chips and motioning him to follow her to the dining room. "I felt a little young to be having children when Fritz came. I remember being wheeled out of the hospital the day after he was born, and I almost wanted to beg the nurses to let me stay. I felt so incompetent— nothing prepared me for the times he would cry and nothing, not food or changing or burping or rocking, would quiet him. But I learned."

"And now do you feel old enough to be his mom?"

"Sometimes I feel *too* old," she admitted.

Although the dining room was a small, cramped room that also served as her office, Trish had done her best to make it a festive place for the evening. While Logan had picked up the food, she had set the table with pretty linen napkins and a vase of some flowers Krysia had given her the day before from the Miller garden.

"You make it look so easy," Logan said, putting down the tray to let her finalize the table arrangements. "I'm a regular kind of bachelor— you know the type, drinks straight from the milk carton if no one's around, never separates the whites from the colors in the wash."

"I used to be that way, before I married Robert. Then I gave my share of dinner parties with paper plates and did too many loads of laundry with the wrong bleach,'' Trish said easily, conveniently minimizing her early efforts and downplaying how much anxiety had gone into correcting her mistakes until she'd been able to play all the roles that wife and mother demanded. ''You've never been married?''

''You can tell, huh?'' Logan asked playfully. ''You're right. Never married, never even lived with a woman. But I can't say that I remember my own mom doing much entertaining, either.''

''Where is Mom now?''

''Both parents are dead,'' he said, acknowledging her reflexive condolence. ''They were quite a bit older when they got married.''

''Brothers and sisters?'' Trish asked, her attention momentarily captured by the wondrous food before her. Had she really not eaten anything since the piece of toast she'd grabbed on the run this morning?

''I have one brother.''

There was a sudden chill in the room, an unnatural silence.

''Oh, I see,'' Trish said, uncertain what emotional minefield she had stepped into.

''He's in prison,'' Logan said abruptly.

''Prison?'' Trish repeated.

"Prison. Five to ten. Armed robbery. He was, maybe he still is, an addict. He's not somebody I'm proud to call a relative."

"Is he why you became a police officer?" Trish asked.

"No," Logan said, shaking his head. "I became a cop right out of high school. I always wanted it, even when I was a kid—I guess I never outgrew the stage where kids divide the world into bad guys and good guys. Bill is only a year younger than me. He was always a bad kid."

"Always?"

Logan shrugged his shoulders and looked away.

"Some kids get into a lot of trouble when they're young. Pranks, bullying, seeing how far they can push the limits, having a chip on their shoulder. Most kids end up on the right path, or someone takes their hand and puts them there. Bill never did. He graduated to being a petty criminal about the same time he graduated from high school. Things went downhill from there."

"Do you visit him?" she asked gently.

"Never," he said vehemently. "In fact, when he got brought into the station here in Hubbard

Woods, I never visited him, never contacted him. I watched the case from a distance.''

"You were ashamed of him?''

''Not that so much as feeling very betrayed by him, almost as if it had been a slap in the face. And it was. He was always trying to prove that he was better than me, or that he was stronger than me. Always competing. Well, he sure proved himself. He destroyed our relationship and he broke my parents' hearts the day he got brought in. He was a lowlife then, and I guess he always will be. So, sometimes I feel like I don't even have family.''

"What if he changes in prison?'' Trish asked. "What if he comes to you and says that he's a new man?''

"I'm not sure that I would believe him,'' Logan admitted. "Because he's certainly said those words time and again when he needed me or my parents to pull him out of a jam. Do you really believe people can change?''

Trish sipped her drink and considered this.

"I think if you don't believe in people being essentially good and people being able to change, you might lose something special inside yourself,'' she said carefully. "Not just you. Anybody.''

"Even you?" Logan challenged.

"Even me," Trish agreed. "But I'm not very good at it. I lost track of the idea that people were decent and that life was good the night Robert was killed. It was so random, it was so undeserved, it was so wrong. *He* had done nothing wrong, and yet he was killed because he went to pick up a quart of milk at the grocery store at ten at night. Just because he was in the wrong place at the wrong time."

"Did they ever catch the murderer?"

Trish shook her head.

"So I have to somehow learn to forgive someone who has no face, someone who has no name, someone who's never seen justice and probably never will. And, if I don't learn to forgive, I can never move on. Even Fritz has that task ahead of him."

"Lady, if you can forgive that person, I admire you a lot."

"I'm not saying I've done it," Trish said. "I haven't. I sometimes feel exactly like Fritz—like I want revenge. But that desire will make me a second victim of the man who pulled the trigger on my husband."

"And you think I need to forgive my brother?"

"I'm really making a fool of myself, telling you what to do with your life...."

"That's what friends do."

Trish studied his face. Had she gone too far? And yet, seeing him here before her, his face lit by candlelight, she felt passionately that he was a stone that could melt. The stern and angry man who had once upset her so much wasn't the real Logan Powell. Beneath the layers of anger at his brother was another man.

"Don't you think that not reaching out to your brother makes you a hardened person inside?" Trish asked. "I mean, when I first met you in Fritz's class, I thought of you as too tough on kids. Now, I just think you're too tough on yourself."

"That's a necessary facade you're looking at, one that every police officer has," Logan defended. "You *have* to be a little rough around the edges, or you'll never be able to stand it. But there can still be a core of humanity—maybe there has to be. You can be at a murder scene, joking with your buddies, with the victim not even five feet away. But there's a part of you that's still reachable. It's not gone."

"Maybe you're right. I was brought down to the morgue when my husband was killed," Trish

said. "A group of officers were eating dough-
nuts and drinking coffee. They were discussing
a football game. At the time, I thought they were
very disrespectful, but maybe they had to be that
way to get through that night."

"And the next night, and the night after that,"
Logan said softly.

"A cop never gets to let it go, does he?"

Logan shook his head sadly.

"Cops still cry, they still have feelings. A
month before my brother was arrested, I got
called to a house where the boyfriend of a
mother had beaten her three-year-old to death
because the kid had wet his pants. I remember
holding my hand to the dead boy's chest. I could
feel the warmth, still there even though the little
boy was gone. I sat there with the murderer
handcuffed a foot away from me and I sobbed
like a baby, feeling the chill making that warm
spot on the kid's chest get smaller and smaller."

Trish gasped at the scene he described.

"But, a month later, my brother destroyed
whatever softness was left in me, the part that
could cry," Logan said. "Because he made me
realize that people like that are the rule, not the
exception."

"Then how can you go back?" Trish asked. "The work you do is destroying you."

She stopped, unable to believe that she would presume to tell him what to do. And yet, her words didn't feel so much like an unwanted challenge as they were an outstretched hand that she knew she had to offer to a drowning man.

"I can't think of anything else," Logan said adamantly. "I have to go back. There's no other life for me than that of a cop. I might have gone into it with a wide-eyed optimism, with a naive desire to help others. But, Trish, you have to understand—I'm a cop, through and through. There's no other life for me. There's nothing else I've ever wanted."

Trish realized more firmly than ever before the gulf that existed between them. For her, Hubbard Woods was a refuge, a permanent answer to the horrors of a world gone mad. For Logan, it was only a stopping point, a brief sabbatical before he placed himself once again on the firing line.

She knew it was important that there be people like him to do their best at protecting the world, at protecting her and her son.

But she couldn't be a part of that struggle.

"Hey, that burrito grande is getting cold,"

Logan pointed out, clearly searching—as she was—for a way back from the stark truths of their conversation. "It's great food. You know, Hubbard Woods hasn't really had a good restaurant before Felicia's opened up."

"You're right," Trish agreed. "Except you'd get an argument from Fritz—he thinks the Cheese-to-Please Pizzeria is just great!"

As the final credits rolled on the comedy, Logan threw his spoon into the empty ice-cream container. He looked over to see Trish sewing the final stitches on a tear on Fritz's favorite pair of jeans. Logan was certain that he hadn't had such a relaxing evening in his life.

And he wasn't sure he wanted it to end.

He had felt no pressure, no sense that he was being judged in that way that women sometimes had—appraising him as a potential lover. She'd made it clear that she valued his friendship, but that that was as far as she wanted the relationship to go. And he found that refreshing, even as he wondered what it would be like to run his fingers through her hair or kiss her rounded lips.

After a shudderingly close conversation about his brother, talk had quickly turned to lighter topics. A movie, the restaurant's dessert on pretty china and then a second dessert of ice cream straight out of the carton. They had stopped the video several times to let Trish finish the laundry and her attention to her chores had reminded them both that this was definitely—no doubt about it—not a date.

He'd had his share of romances, affairs, relationships—whatever they could be called. Mostly with cop groupies, the women who loved the sense of danger from a safe distance that came with making love to the uniform. The women who loved the feel of his leather jacket with its Chicago flag sewn on the sleeve. The women who wanted to hear every detail of every night's shift, until a guy got to feeling that it wasn't him she was interested in so much as the adventure. The women who drifted, at the breakup, into a buddy's arms. The women who made it easy, very easy, on him. He had never had to pursue, never had to change anything about himself, never had to accommodate, to get the simply physical gratification.

He hadn't needed that kind of relationship in a long time, but he hadn't known what to replace it with.

Now he knew.

"How about a few minutes of the news?" he asked, punching the Eject button on the VCR.

Trish looked up from her work with a smile.

"All right," she said. "But then I'm afraid I'm going to have to throw you out. I'm already past my bedtime."

"Fritz must get you up pretty early in the morning."

The phone rang, and Trish leapt to get it. Logan turned off the television.

"Yes...that poor boy...I'll be right there."

"He needs to come home?" Logan asked, as she hung up.

"Yeah, Paul fell asleep about twenty minutes ago, but Fritz can't seem to settle down and wants to bail out."

Logan was already up and in his jacket.

"How 'bout I walk you over and see you guys home safely?"

"That's a nice offer," she said. "Are you sure you don't have someplace else to be?"

"Lady, there's nothing more exciting than a hamperful of laundry waiting for me."

She laughed and slipped into the Windbreaker that he held out for her.

Although it was late and the air crisply cold, there were still a few patrons of Felicia's congregating on the sidewalk, window-shopping by the clear light of the street lamps while waiting for a table. Logan and Trish briskly passed them, and headed away from the quaint stores. On the residential block where the Millers lived, the moonlight was dimmed by the sprawling trees. The Miller house was ablaze with lights.

Krysia waited on the front steps of the house, with Fritz seated beside her, backpack and teddy bear in hand. Trish quickened her steps.

"It's all right, he just got a little worried," Krysia said as Fritz tiredly slumped into his mother's arms. "With Paul asleep and the girls involved in a marathon gossip session, the party wasn't quite as much fun."

"How are you?" Trish asked her son.

"I'm fine," Fritz said defiantly. "I just want my own bed."

"Okay, tiger," Logan said, coming up to the porch and exchanging a quick greeting with Krysia. "You want me to carry you?"

Fritz nodded, and held himself out to be hoisted onto Logan's shoulders. Trish gathered up his backpack and teddy.

"Sorry," she said to Krysia.

"Nothing to be sorry about," her friend answered. "The boys had a great time. They'll do it again—they've got the rest of their childhood, remember? We're not going anywhere, and I get the impression you're anxious to stay in Hubbard Woods, too. Just remember, Lizzie went on three—or maybe it was four—sleep overs at her best friend's house before she got the hang of it. Now they're inseparable.''

"And Lizzie's sixteen," Trish said. "She has a lifelong friend."

"Exactly," Krysia said. "Hey, is something wrong?"

Trish looked back at the sidewalk, where Logan held Fritz in his arms, barely visible under the shadow of a large oak.

"No, nothing's wrong," she muttered. "Listen, thanks."

"Sure. Now, I'll pick up Fritz tomorrow around ten to go to the pancake house for breakfast. The boys'll still want that, I'm sure."

"Okay." Trish nodded.

"Hey, don't take it so hard," Krysia said, putting a hand on her shoulder. "It's not a big deal at all. Kids have to go through this...."

"It's nothing," Trish said. "I'm just a little tired myself, I guess."

"I'll call just before I leave for your apartment tomorrow morning."

"Okay, thanks, good night."

Trish walked back to the sidewalk. Fritz had already fallen asleep, burying soft snores into Logan's shoulder.

She couldn't shake the terrible chill she'd felt as Krysia had gently, so casually mapped out a future for Fritz and Paul.

Oh, it was the future she wanted. A best friend whose house was close enough to walk to. A neighborhood where people were friendly. A park nearby where boyhood adventures would flourish. A school she could respect. A future for Fritz opened up before her, filled with love and warmth—

But, at that moment, more vividly than she could bear, she realized that it had no place in it for Logan.

Because Logan's world was…back there. On the force, in the dead of night, among people who had no respect for life, with danger at every corner. It was a world Logan would be returning to, because he had no choice.

Trish understood that Logan had no choice. He *had* to be on the force. She understood that, even if she also believed that Logan didn't see so clearly the connection between his tenacious hold on police work and his sense of betrayal at his brother's hands.

She knew, so clearly that it made a sour taste in her mouth as they walked silently back into the light, back into the reach of the chattering customers of the popular restaurant—she knew that Logan and she could be the most casual of friends, no more. And soon it would be even less. When he returned to Chicago, to the police force.

He followed her upstairs to the apartment and laid Fritz on his bed, watching silently as she pulled the covers protectively up around her son's shoulders.

"I'd better throw you out now," she said, deciding that it was probably best not to invite him to watch any of the news or drink any coffee. "I had a wonderful time tonight."

"Say 'hello' to him and tell him I'll see him on Tuesday, regular class," Logan said, and she wondered if he, too, sensed how quickly their friendship was ending.

Chapter Seven

"Now, I want each of you to extend your left hand and hold back your right," Logan announced. Craning his neck over his shoulder as he demonstrated his words, he surveyed the line of boys, each with their left hand held high.

Except one.

"Paul, switch your hands," he ordered.

The youngster, flustered, jerked his right hand back and flung out his left so that the line-up was perfectly matched.

Well, as perfectly matched as twenty five-year-olds can be, Logan thought to himself. They were doing pretty good for the end of the class, when attentions wander and tired boys fidget. His own attention had been wandering as he, too, felt tired.

He'd had to make a conscious effort not to let his gaze settle on the bleachers, toward the back, where Trish sat.

"All right, good job," he said. "Now relax."

Arms dropped to their sides, the boys looked expectantly at their *Sensei*.

"Feet on the red line," he exclaimed, pointing to the basketball court center line. When the class had settled into place, Logan bowed to his students.

The boys solemnly bowed in return.

At least this was the part of karate that all of them could do well.

Logan clapped his hands, signaling the end of the lesson.

"Great class!" he shouted.

The boys shrieked with the release of their pent-up energy and raced for their shoes. Some struggled against the knots in their white belts. Their mothers held up jackets and searched for errant socks.

It had been a tough day. He had taught five classes, forty-five minutes each, back-to-back without a break. His muscles ached, reminding him of every one of his thirty-five years.

He walked over to the bleachers, seeking out Trish and Fritz.

"How did I do?" Fritz asked, looking up from watching his mother, who was crouched at his feet struggling with the laces of his shoes.

"You did wonderfully," Logan said honestly. "But I need to talk to your mom."

"Uh-oh, is it a good talk or a bad talk with Mom?"

"What do you mean—good talk or bad talk?"

"Well, sometimes when you've talked with Mom, it's meant trouble."

Trish looked up at Logan and, as their eyes met, he felt a quick *thaddump!* in his chest.

Dehydration, he told himself quickly. Better drink a lot of water. He hadn't had a chance to catch the drinking fountain since the end of the second class. In addition to making his heart work overtime, dehydration left his throat dusty and dry and hot. Come to think of it, the gym was pretty warm. No fans. And the air was heavy with humidity. It had *nothing* to do with the fact Trish was looking at him.

Trouble, huh? Maybe so.

But to Fritz, he merely said, "Good talk."

Trish stood up.

"Is there something wrong?"

Logan shook his head. He motioned her to the center of the gym, the calm eye in a hurricane of activity.

"I just need a favor from you," he said. "Nothing special. No big deal. Nothing at all."

"Okay," she said with the slightest touch of wariness. "What is it?"

He hesitated, feeling his mouth lose the last little bit of moisture. His tongue felt like several cotton balls had been glued to it. His heart felt like it was struggling with the last steps of the 100-yard dash. His hands felt clammy with sweat. Baffled by his mounting physical discomfort, he started to speak, and then stopped. His legs weakened ever so slightly.

This schedule is killing me, he thought, and then he took a deep breath, concentrating on the rhythms of his body the way he had been taught in the Chicago *dojo* where he had learned karate as well as the ancient arts of meditation.

But the *sensei*s and wise men of ancient Japan had never been face-to-face with Trish Eastman.

"Logan, are you all right?"

He looked into her eyes, those eyes that he

had seen last night. And the night before. And the night before that.

Every morning he had been awakening from a dream that he couldn't remember, but which tugged at him throughout the day. And while the details of the dream still eluded him, he knew that she was a part of it, her eyes beckoning him.

Standing before her, he knew, with blinding clarity, exactly what was making his body fall apart. It was enough to make him laugh, if he hadn't, after all, been so shook up.

Logan Powell, who had faced down some of the most cold-blooded criminals.

Logan Powell, who had more than once taken a bullet and then covered over his fears with emergency room jokes.

Logan Powell, who had a collection of commendation awards for bravery that would be the envy of any officer.

Logan Powell was scared.

"I've got this thing I have to go to," he said, feeling his words stick to those pesky cotton balls on his tongue. "The Parent-Teacher Board Annual Dinner is on Friday. I'd like you to go with me. Be my escort. As a favor."

As soon as it was out of his mouth, he felt his

equilibrium return. At least he could breathe without thinking that his chest would explode.

This wasn't the first formal dinner he had attended. Nor was it the first event with suits he'd been invited to where a woman on his arm was a necessity. In the past, he'd asked his former squad car partner, Norene McWilliams, who had gone on to become a Community Service Liaison. She'd also called Logan when there was something special she had to attend. He was a great no-hassle companion. So was she. No big deal.

But Norene's boyfriend had returned from his post in Germany and they were married now. She had Charlie to escort her and, while both Norene and Charlie might be very understanding, Logan just wasn't comfortable with asking Norene to accompany him any longer. It just didn't feel right to step out with a married woman on his arm.

Logan had nobody he could turn to, except an ex-girlfriend from many years back—if he could find her phone number—or maybe the dispatcher from his precinct who was rumored to have a crush on him. In any case, he didn't want to ask either of them because he didn't want to raise their expectations or make promises he couldn't keep.

Or maybe it was just that Trish was the first person he'd thought of when he'd received his engraved invitation and the congratulatory call from the chairman of the PTB.

He had actually thought it was a rather brilliant idea to ask Trish. She would look good next to him, she knew how to act with people, and she might even make the evening a little less stilted—the same cold, clean criteria he had used when asking Norene and Norene had used when asking him.

It was as simple as that, right?

He certainly hadn't had this physical reaction when he had asked Norene to go to the union's cocktail party. He was positive Norene hadn't had this reaction when she'd asked him to go with her to the Urban League Community Service Night six months ago, just before Charlie got back.

"A dinner?" Trish asked.

His breath caught. He suddenly realized—she might say no.

"Cocktails and dinner," he clarified, shifting his weight from one foot to another. "And some speeches, hopefully brief, afterward. On Friday.''

I'm acting like a teenager asking a girl on a first date, he thought, mentally kicking himself. Except he hadn't had this kind of trouble even when he was a teen. Logan Powell didn't have a problem asking women out. He had done his share with ease, and, as a result of the modern age, had been asked out by women even more often.

Maybe I'm just out of practice, he rationalized, remembering that it had been quite some time since he'd made the effort to get involved with a woman—even if only for one night.

The further he got into this conversation, the more he realized that Trish Eastman was anything but safe. She wasn't exactly what he would call a no-complications date.

''I…guess I could go,'' Trish said, hesitating a split second too long for Logan's taste. ''I'll ask Krysia to baby-sit Fritz.''

''Great,'' Logan said, feeling something akin to sunshine wash over him. ''I'll pick you up around six-thirty.''

As Trish left the gym with Fritz, as a mother approached him to ask about registration for the next month's session, as he headed for the locker room, he felt lighter. The backs of his legs didn't ache. The muscles in his neck didn't feel so tight. His headache had disappeared and he just wasn't as tired as he'd thought he was. He got a drink at the fountain and the water tasted better—clearer and fresher—than he had remembered.

Catching his reflection in the mirror as he neared his locker, he started.

He saw the face of a happy man.

The happy man was a stranger to Logan, and he rubbed his hand against his jaw, noting how the muscles in his face were relaxed. He studied the eyes, how the tiny wrinkles at their corners had disappeared, leaving the lightest of tan lines.

Suddenly he straightened, his eyes narrowing at his reflection.

"Oh, no, buddy, don't do this to me," he warned himself.

But sternness was no match for the smiling self on the other side of the glass. That self ignored his own inner voice that told him that happiness, joy and delight were all things that belonged to other people. That Logan Powell was simply a guardian for other people's happiness, never to enjoy it guiltlessly himself.

On the street in half an hour, he whistled a

tune that had been popular when he was a teen-ager. He stopped at the Sweet Shoppe and bought a quarter pound of Gummi Bear can-dies—and popped several in his mouth before he even remembered that he didn't like candy. He waved cheerily to the owner of the grocery store and helped a woman with several heavy bags get her things loaded into the trunk of her car.

He walked toward the bridge over the train tracks. A commuter train had just pulled into the station, letting off gray-suited men and a few women. A parade of cars waited in the parking lot to pick them up.

Logan paused, standing at the railing of the bridge to watch the commuter procession.

He watched a child and mother, standing at the station house door, searching the crowd of commuters. The child broke away, recognizing his daddy and raced into the protection and warmth of his arms. Unaware he was doing so, Logan bit his lip so hard that he felt the salty taste explode within him.

He turned away as the man, carrying his child, met the child's mother for a kiss, their family complete as they embraced.

Logan wasn't a teen asking for a first date anymore.

As much as he wanted the fresh joy of discovery that comes with romance, he was thirty-five years old and he needed to be practical. Realistic. Pragmatic.

There were consequences to being involved with a woman.

And the consequences with Trish could only be heartache.

For one of them, for both of them, maybe even for the three of them when he realized that he had to think of Fritz.

In fact, it was safest to think of Fritz's feelings, because there was nothing he wouldn't do to prevent that child from hurting. Sacrificing his momentary feelings of attraction to Trish to protect Fritz was easy.

He could let himself have a good time at the dinner, and enjoy himself on Friday night, but he had to rein in his feelings. He had to remember that acting on his impulses like a teenager wasn't an option for him.

A lot of his classmates in the Academy weren't on the force anymore.

Some of them had left because they were frustrated. Some had left because the pay was so low. Some had left because they were forced to—the ones who used the badge as a shield for their brutality.

But even more had left because of a woman.

A woman who couldn't stay up nights waiting for a phone call that meant injury or death.

And those cops ended up with great suits and briefcases and wallets filled with pictures of the wife and children they loved.

But Logan had always felt sorry for them because they each, in their own way, had given up something special. Logan was never going to leave. Not for the money. Not for the frustrations on the job, which he accepted.

Not for a woman.

"That's not you, pal," he said out loud.

As he continued on his way, he noticed that the back of his legs hurt. Maybe he had pulled a muscle, he thought to himself distractedly.

Cinderella didn't have to dress a five-year-old on the night of the ball and she certainly didn't spend twenty minutes looking for Fritz Eastman's shoes so he could be walked over to Krysia Miller's house.

Cinderella didn't have to stitch up the side

seams of her dress because a year of mourning had dropped ten pounds from her body.

Cinderella didn't have hair that wouldn't, just wouldn't, stay put, but instead pulled out of an amateur chignon defiantly. Didn't her fairy godmother take care of all that?

Rifling through her closet looking for a purse that would go with the off-the-shoulder black velvet dress she had chosen—one that was better than her everyday fanny pack—made her wish that she did have that fairy godmother. To find her keys. To put up her hair. To have walked Fritz over to the Miller house earlier in the afternoon.

On the other hand, at least Trish didn't have to get nervous about meeting a prince.

So there wasn't much she had in common with the fairy-tale heroine, except when Logan Powell walked into the apartment wearing a jet black tuxedo. Cinderella might have bitten her nails, too. Because there was something very nerve-racking about Logan Powell looking like a prince.

"Wow," he said with boyish, reverent awe when he saw her. "I feel like I have to watch it or I'll get turned into a footman or something."

"That was the lizard," Trish said, laughing. "The dog was changed into a footman."

"Oh, yeah," he said, and then his face became serious. "Trish, you look...stunning."

As his eyes registered his pleasure at her dramatic transformation, Trish heard the warning voice within her.

Oh, God, don't let him look at me like this—I can't handle this. Not right now. Not from him.

Too dangerous.

Did Cinderella ever feel this way?

If Trish was smart, she would push him out the door of her apartment. She would take off the dress, forget finding her keys, curl up in a sweat suit and watch the Friday night lineup of sitcoms.

But he was holding her keys and her shawl—a wrap of soft, black cashmere that she had laid out on the couch in preparation for this moment. She didn't have a clue how to gracefully, or even not so gracefully, back out of dinner.

"We've got to run," he said. "Cocktails started four minutes ago."

He put her wrap around her shoulders, and Trish wondered if it was her imagination at work when she felt his hands linger. They hadn't touched since their one hug, and Trish had felt her mind drawn back time and again to thoughts of his touch so frequently, against her wishes, that she nearly felt the imprint of his hands.

She was at war with herself as she looked up at him, and felt herself both inviting and pushing away the electric impulses.

"It's four blocks to the hotel," Logan said. "Would you like to walk, or would it be too hard on your heels?"

Trish looked down briefly at her black *peau de soie* pumps. Cinderella rode in a carriage, but would she have been happier with a stroll to the palace?

"No, let's not take a car," she answered. "I can't get enough of window-shopping and seeing the leaves now that they've turned colors."

"You're like me," Logan said. "I've spent the last four months walking every inch of this town. Even though I grew up here, so much has changed."

They walked down to the sidewalk. As they crossed Chestnut Street, Logan took her arm when she stumbled very lightly on the gravel. It had been, by her count, at least a year since she had worn heels and she was grateful for his help across the street.

And yet, as she felt the pressure of his arm

against hers, she wondered if the casual intimacy was a signal that the relationship was veering off into dangerous territory.

"I can't tell you how thankful I am that you're coming tonight," Logan said. They'd paused briefly in front of the Book Stall window. "I don't like doing this sort of thing by myself. I owe you one."

Oh, so that was it, Trish thought, feeling as if she'd been splashed with cold water. A favor, he'd said when he had asked her.

"I owe you one."

Friends did favors for each other. Friends owed each other in that lighthearted way that meant there really wasn't a tally being kept. Friends were thankful for favors, grateful for help, quick with their acknowledgements.

She relaxed, knowing that at least this Cinderella didn't have a prince. *Couldn't* have a prince in her life, if that prince wouldn't provide safety and security to her son.

Maybe she was crazy, maybe she was wrong, maybe she was only fooling herself, but she still thought they could be friends—at least for the little while before Logan got called back to his duty.

Couldn't they?

Chapter Eight

The party-goers, sipping white wine and munching on appetizers, had spilled from the cozy reception room into the wide hallway on the second floor of the Hubbard Woods Commons Inn. Trish and Logan heard the insistent murmur of the crowd as they walked up the grand staircase, but neither was prepared for the crush of bodies as they reached the hallway.

"My God," Logan muttered. "If I had known, I would have refused."

"Refused to come?" Trish asked.

"No, I guess I forgot to tell you," Logan said sheepishly. "I'm getting an award. In fact, that's the purpose of the evening. I'll be given an award after the dinner—I'm the Parent-Teacher Board Volunteer of the Year. Hope you don't mind all the fuss.''

Hope you don't mind? She looked up at him, surprised. If she was the honored guest at a dinner for two hundred, she would be sure to say something about it. She wouldn't be able to stop herself.

But studying him now she realized that he felt genuinely abashed by the idea of being honored. Did he think he didn't deserve any recognition for the work that he did? She wondered at the kind of demons that would make a man feel this way.

"Logan! Logan Powell, I'm so delighted you're here!'' a woman exclaimed, emerging from the crowd. She took his hand. "Libby Joyce, president of the Parents' Board. We met at the Parent/Child Seminar night. Come on, I have so many people who are dying to meet you.''

She pulled at him, urging him forward into the sea of people. But Logan held firm, turning to Trish and refusing to let her slip away as she would have preferred.

"Come on," he whispered. "This is where I really need you."

He tugged on her arm and she followed. They squeezed their way through the guests, trying to keep up with Libby.

"Isn't your son in Mrs. Meadows's class?" A voice called brightly in Trish's ear.

Trish turned reflexively and came face-to-face with a woman she recognized as the mother of one of Fritz's classmates. The woman was wearing a sequin-studded dress and appeared as comfortable in the glamorous party atmosphere as she did in her sweats at the door of Hubbard Woods Elementary.

"Yes, I'm Fritz's mom," Trish said. "Trish Eastman."

Logan was slipping away, being pulled through the crowd so that her only contact with him was his hand, which would soon lose its grip on her.

"I'm Sally," the woman said. "You're here with Logan Powell, aren't you?"

Trish nodded, feeling Logan's hand tug insistently, having only enough time to catch the look of open admiration that Sally gave Logan before she was enveloped by the crowd. As Logan led her through the path of the reception, Trish noted the other women. They stared at him, even if only for a second taken away from concentrating on the person with whom they spoke. He attracted attention from people of both sexes as he passed, and Trish felt herself drawn to study him. To really look at him in a way that she had avoided since they had first met.

He was handsome, that she already knew. But she hadn't come to grips with the fact that he was the sort of man who made heads turn—women with admiration, men with a sort of wary respect. He filled out his tuxedo in an almost primitive way. One that made clear that civilization might have required him to dress, but inside he wasn't tamed in the slightest. He was apart from them all, a member of a larger world that relied on his strengths. The same strengths that these guests could only intuit, but which they needed—from someone—to protect them.

And yet, she knew without any doubt that he had no idea how others looked at him.

Though women repeatedly tried to catch his eye, he was utterly unaware of their admiration. When one woman in a brilliant pink cocktail dress leaned over to take his arm and brightly introduce herself as the mother of one of his students, Trish noticed that he graciously smiled but didn't even acknowledge the clearly predatory feminine intentions.

Libby Joyce stopped at a circle of six older men and women who had congregated near the stained-glass windows that caught the last light of the day. Logan stood beside her and nodded at those he recognized.

"Here's the star of our evening," Libby said to the group, catching their attention. "Logan Powell from the Gang Crimes Unit in Chicago. Logan, I'd like to introduce you to some of the members of the school board whom you haven't already…"

"And Trish Eastman," Logan interrupted, pulling Trish to his side and putting his arm around her waist.

"Oh, pardon me," Libby said, extending her hand to Trish. "I'm sorry, but I can't remember your connection with Logan?"

Trish opened her mouth to speak and then could not think what to say. Friends? Just friends—not lovers.

Definitely not lovers.

"Trish is a mother from right here in Hubbard Woods," Logan supplied. "She's kind enough to put up with me tonight."

One of the men chuckled loudly at the ambiguous explanation that explained nothing. The small group widened to let her in as Logan reached to a passing waiter and got a glass of wine for himself and her.

Trish was grateful for his determination to make her a part of things, even though she felt uncomfortable with the attention. The group politely questioned Trish about how she liked Hubbard Woods and how Fritz was adjusting to the community. Libby, remembering her now, commented about the delicious brownies she had made for the last Parent/Child Seminar, but Trish was grateful when the conversation's focus shifted.

"Logan, we've heard a lot about your programs, especially the ones for kids," Paul Nilson, chairman of the board, said. "Would you, by any chance, consider leaving the force in order to do these programs on a regular basis throughout the North Shore suburbs?"

"Absolutely not," Logan replied. "My first love is police work, and I'll be returning to the force as soon as I'm able. Besides, running these programs for school districts would take business and organizational skills I just don't have."

Trish sipped her wine and looked at Logan as if she were simply listening to the normal, light patter of cocktail parties. But his words, spoken with a passion that she knew ran deep, reminded her that his days in Hubbard Woods were coming to a close. Their friendship—brief and delicate—would fade.

"It's too bad you won't reconsider," Paul said. "There's a real need for somebody to take these kids and show them that drugs, gangs and crime are wrong. You have a real gift, young man. One that not many people have."

"You must be a helluva cop," another man said. "I sat in on the program you did last week for the sixth-graders at Kenilworth Elementary. If you're as good on the streets as you are with those children, I think it's great you'll be back on the force."

Logan winced at the lavish praise, but then recovered.

"I better get back to my job," he said with a twinkle in his eye. "There's nothing on the streets that's as frightening as the kids from the Kenilworth district!"

The group chuckled at his humor and the conversation passed to more general topics. But Trish felt herself watching him as he joined the laughter at a joke about an unpopular politician. He leaned down to hear more clearly an anec-

dote from an elderly woman and he unconsciously brushed an errant lock of hair back from
his forehead.

She was going to miss him.

He had become so much a part of her life and
of her thoughts. Even of her dreams, if she remembered things correctly in the cold light of
this very morning. She would miss him, and yet,
it was probably best that he was leaving—moving back downtown and immersing himself in
the life and work that he loved so much. She
would have to let go, and letting go was always
difficult, whether it was letting go of a husband
who had been shot down or the bittersweet letting go of a son old enough to walk to school
on his own or ride his bicycle around the block
without a parent beside him.

This, too, would be difficult but she would do
it.

And so she smiled and laughed and listened
attentively at all the right times. Within minutes
the doors to the dining room were opened and
the lights in the reception room dimmed as a
signal to guests that dinner was to be served.

"We're seated at the head table," Logan said,
taking her arm. "Sorry I didn't warn you."

"If you had, I might have declined," Trish

said lightly. "After all, I could have spent the evening with the laundry and Fritz and a pizza delivered by Cheese-to-Please."

"That does sound like a much better time, doesn't it?" Logan asked.

Trish looked up at him quickly, and realized that, while she had been joking, at least, a little, he was utterly serious.

"Come on, Logan, this is your special night," she said, squeezing his arm. "You're being honored because these people really need you. You're helping their children and there's nothing people want more than security for their kids."

"Do you really believe that?"

"That people want a good life for their kids? Of course I do. As much as I believe that you've helped. And you've made a difference for these people's kids. That's why they're here tonight."

They reached the head table and found their seats, side by side near the central podium. He held out her chair and gently draped her shawl over the back of it as she sat down.

"I think they're here tonight—" he said, pausing to survey the glittering array of tables laden with fine china and silverware, the waiters pouring wine into the fluted glasses, the guests exchanging greetings with their table mates. "I think they're here tonight because there's a party.''

There was no mistaking the sadness in his voice.

''I'm sure that having a nice party has something to do with it,'' Trish said. ''But, is it so hard to believe that they're also here because they want to say thank-you? How can you deny the gratitude they feel?''

Logan shrugged uncomfortably and looked away just as a waiter appeared to place salads in front of them and pour wine into the empty glasses in front of them.

The man who was seated at Trish's other side introduced himself and quickly monopolized her attention as he cataloged his successes as a businessman. She noticed that Logan was similarly taken over by the woman to his right, who touched his forearm every time she made a point. Logan had no visible response to the woman's clearly seductive designs.

''You've hardly touched your food,'' Logan whispered to Trish as plates from the main course—beef Wellington with baby carrots— were whisked away.

''I find it hard to eat in a fishbowl,'' Trish confessed. ''Sitting here at the head table is very hard for me—I feel like everybody's staring at me."

"People do stare," Logan said. "But you get used to it."

"You're not eating, either," Trish pointed out.

"That's because I have to give a talk afterward. I don't like to speak on a full stomach."

"Nervous?"

"A little. Okay, a lot."

"But you're very good at public speaking."

"That may be. But I'm not very good at awards," Logan said, leaning back to allow a waiter to place the cheesecake dessert in front of him. "How 'bout a hamburger at Hubbard Woods Grill later tonight?"

She hesitated, ready to say no, she should make an early night of it. Then she looked at his eyes. He needed to look forward to a lighthearted, casual dinner.

He needed her.

It was a startling thought, because so much of their relationship had been focused on what he could do for her, mostly by helping Fritz. She'd never thought of herself as having anything special to offer to Logan.

She'd never thought of Logan as needy.

And yet, he was. He could be brave, he could be strong, but he couldn't accept the rewards of bravery and strength.

"I'll have to check with Krysia first, to see how Fritz is doing," Trish said. "But if he's okay, I'd be delighted to."

Trish didn't even have a chance to push her slice of cheesecake around on her plate before Paul Nilson rose and approached the podium. The dining room quieted. Waiters silently roamed the hall, pouring coffee into diners' cups.

"We are very lucky to have as our Volunteer of the Year a very special man who grew up in Hubbard Woods," Paul began. "Logan Powell left our small community to become an officer with the Chicago Police Department. He rose quickly through the ranks, becoming the youngest detective in the force and later becoming one of the founders of the Gang Crimes Unit."

Trish sneaked a peak at Logan. His face was flushed—almost as if he were embarrassed—and he was focusing on studying his cheesecake.

"Though he has become a successful police officer," Paul continued, "Logan has never forgotten the community from which he came. Over the years, he has returned to Hubbard

Woods time and again to teach our children about the dangers of drugs, gangs and crime. When he was recently placed on an extended leave as a result of an on-the-job injury, Logan came back to live in Hubbard Woods. He has spent the time which should have been used for some well-deserved rest to volunteer his time teaching karate at the Community House, putting on numerous anticrime programs at every level of the schools, and consulting with our teachers and administrators on potential problems developing within our community. We owe an enormous debt of gratitude to him—and that's why we, the Parent-Teacher Board, are pleased to give him our annual Volunteer of the Year award!''

The room erupted in applause and everyone rose to their feet. Trish stood and felt her heart swell with emotion as Logan approached the podium. Clearly ill at ease with the attention, he nonetheless projected a self-confidence that made it possible for him to shake hands with Paul as he was given a gold plaque, wave to several people he knew, and reach out to take the hands of those who clamored for the opportunity to touch him. It was several minutes before the room quieted, and during those minutes, Trish saw him as others saw him.

As a hero.

A hero who was a hero even when he was just sitting in a classroom with a bunch of kids. A hero who was a hero even when he wasn't chasing criminals or making arrests. A hero who was a hero just for being himself, for caring the way he did, for teaching the way he did.

It's too bad he can't see himself this way, too, Trish thought as the applause died down and everyone returned to their seats.

"I can't tell you what it means to be recognized in this way," Logan said, holding aloft his plaque. "Hubbard Woods is a wonderful place in which to grow up, to raise a family, to feel some shelter from the problems of the rest of the world. And it takes all of us, working together, to carve out that safety. *I* owe Hubbard Woods, not the other way around. And I don't think I'll ever be able to repay the community."

"Ha! He'll never be able to repay Hubbard Woods for the damage his brother did," the man next to Trish whispered.

Trish stared at the man, horrified that he would say such a thing.

She looked at Logan, but he was continuing

with his speech and Trish was certain he hadn't heard the rude remark.

"What did his brother do that was so bad?" Trish asked quietly.

"Nothing major," the man replied. "Just an accumulation of petty crimes and juvenile hijinks. He was trouble right from the start—I heard he's in prison, now. Too bad he was so different from Logan. I figure Logan will be trying to make up for his brother for the rest of his life."

Trying to make up for his brother for the rest of his life.

The man turned away, caught up by the laughter of the audience at an anecdote Logan had shared with them. Trish looked at the audience, at the rapt attention the guests gave to Logan. The words of the man seated next to her echoed in her head. *Trying to make up for his brother....*

She gulped at her too-hot coffee and pushed herself to listen to Logan's speech.

Logan was a hero...and not even his brother could change that.

Chapter Nine

A quick phone call to Krysia reassured her that another hour spent getting a bite to eat was all right.

"Michael rented them an X-MEN video for after dinner," Krysia explained. "The boys fell asleep after five minutes, but my husband's still in there watching it. Don't worry—if Fritz can sleep through the X-MEN being attacked by the forces of evil, I'm sure he'll sleep long enough for you to get something decent to eat."

After an evening of the finest food but none to eat, Trish thought she would faint with pleasure at the first bite of the double cheeseburger, a specialty of the Hubbard Woods Grill.

"This is great, isn't it?" Logan said, noting her pleasure. "This is what I grew up on. I ruined my appetite here nearly every afternoon during high school—a burger, a large order of fries, a milk shake at four o'clock—and even my mom's baked spaghetti casserole couldn't tempt me."

She looked around the nearly empty diner, imagining a young Logan Powell at the counter or one of the leather-covered booths.

"I could never get away with eating like this every day," Trish said, dipping a french fry in the puddle of ketchup at the side of her plate. "I'd be two hundred pounds."

"Well, I was burning a lot of calories—training in Chicago at a Japanese *dojo* twice a week and practicing for hours every day," Logan said. He regarded his plate thoughtfully. "But, I don't have the metabolism today I did when I was younger, because I know I couldn't eat like this as often, either. We all slow down a little, I guess."

"Not by much, if you're the standard."

"I'm thirty-five and that's old for guys who are still on the streets," Logan admitted. "I can't keep up with the newest recruits. Most of my classmates are taking desk jobs."

"So, what about you? You don't want to have a desk?"

He shook his head. "Not ready yet."

They ate for a few minutes in a comfortable silence.

"I'm glad you came with me tonight," Logan said. "I couldn't have done that by myself. I probably would have bolted in the middle of dinner."

"But you looked so confident."

"I sure didn't feel that way. I didn't like the idea of the award in the first place—but I agreed to it because the money they raise with the dinner goes toward the Parent-Teacher Board's budget."

"And you're very loyal to Hubbard Woods's schools," Trish guessed.

"I am. I really meant what I said tonight about this place being a wonderful place to grow up in. You've moved someplace special, someplace where Fritz has the best possible chance at a good future."

Trish thought of the man who had been seated next to her.

"What about your brother? He was raised here, but things didn't work out in his life."

Logan's eyes narrowed, glinting with anger.

"What made you think of him?"

Trish blushed, ashamed that she had brought up a subject that clearly made him so uncomfortable.

"I shouldn't have said anything. I'm sorry," she apologized. "The man sitting next to me said something about him and I was wondering…"

"I'll never escape him," Logan muttered.

"Why should you need to?"

"He's in prison, for God's sake!"

"But he's still your brother," Trish said. "No matter what—he's still family."

"I wish he wasn't," Logan said darkly. "Okay, maybe that's a little extreme. I just feel ashamed of him. I feel like I'm always making up for him."

The comment made by the man who had sat next to her might not be the way others viewed Logan and his brother. Still, many people who lived in Hubbard Woods would know the two brothers. Logan must think every one of those people blamed him for his brother's crimes.

"He's your brother, but what he chooses to do isn't your responsibility," she said. "Why do you feel like you're the one who has to pay for what he did?"

Logan looked away, his jaw clenched.

"He always had a chip on his shoulder, always wanted to outdo me," he said quietly. "Since he was only a year behind me, beating me at anything—sports, girls, grades—was something nearly but not quite attainable. When we turned into teenagers, he just veered off in the opposite direction from me. As if to say that, if he couldn't beat me, he would simply quit."

"I'm not sure I understand."

"Let me give you one example. I was working harder and harder at karate. Getting good, going to competitions. He tried it for a few years and then dropped out when he realized that I would always be just a little bit ahead of him. You know, when I was four, I can clearly remember he once said 'You just wait until I'm older than you.' Well, that day never came. And it wouldn't come with karate until he could become disciplined enough for practice."

"So he stopped karate."

"Right—just like he quit half a dozen other things. Instead, he did his best to ruin things for me and our parents, drawing attention to himself by acting out. He kept getting into trouble—small stuff like shoplifting at the drugstore or spraying graffiti on the neighbor's garage—and it was always timed so that whenever I was about to achieve anything, he'd be there first,'' Logan said. ''Ruining my special day with a new catastrophe. It all came to a head when I graduated. Top of my class. My brother went joyriding in the principal's wife's car the night before—so on my graduation day, my parents had to shuttle between the police station and the ceremony. And I couldn't look the principal in the eye.''

''But how does this make you feel like you're the one who's to blame?''

''Because I knew, every time I accomplished something, it was like rubbing salt into his wound.''

''So you couldn't achieve anything without thinking it carried a price—your brother getting out of hand.''

''Yes, that's it,'' Logan said. ''And sometimes I would feel guilty about giving him a reason to act like a jerk, and other times I would resent him because he made everything so difficult.''

''And now he's the reason you can't accept the praise and admiration that people give you.''

Logan looked at her sharply. Almost ready to

take back her words, to apologize for being so personal, she stopped when he spoke first.

"You're right," he said. "I thought I would die up there at that podium. I could hear myself giving a speech, talking like I was in a room with two hundred of my closest friends. I don't think anybody knew I was nervous."

"No, they didn't."

"But inside I kept waiting for some disaster, for someone to leap to their feet and say that I didn't deserve this."

"Who would do that?" Trish asked, horrified.

"The man who sat next to you," Logan said quietly. "It was like the day I got my detective badge. It was only a few days after my brother had been picked up for armed robbery. I was half thinking someone would tell me that I didn't deserve it. Because of Bill."

"And you haven't talked to him since."

Logan shook his head.

"His attorney came to me asking me for money to pay his legal bills," Logan said.

"Did you?"

"I did, but with the condition that he never try to contact me again. Even so, he wrote a few letters to me a year ago. I sent them back unopened—I assume he was just asking for money.

I can't change the kind of person he is, and what can I get in return but trouble?''

"Peace of mind,'' Trish said softly.

Logan shook his head.

"Not from him. Not ever. I've made my choice in life and he's made his.''

His vehemence foreclosed any further discussion and Trish was grateful when the waitress brought over a pot of coffee and asked them for their dessert orders. By the time they had settled on sharing a piece of pecan pie and another of cherry, their talk had turned lighter. They discovered they both had a passion for English mystery novels, had watched every episode of "M*A*S*H,'' and had felt like outsiders in high school.

"I can understand why *I* felt that way,'' Logan said. "I was spending all my time learning karate and studying. I didn't spend a lot of time socializing. But, why did you feel that way?''

Trish shrugged and shook her head.

"I felt like a real ugly duckling,'' she explained. "I was too skinny. I wore braces until I was sixteen. And I never knew what to do at parties.''

"Talk to boys like me, that's what you do,'' Logan teased.

"Boys like you were studying," Trish pointed out.

"If I had known there were girls like *you* around," Logan challenged, "I would have known how to make better use of my time."

Trish giggled, but her voice caught as her eyes met his.

The light bantering tone had been changed by the introduction of a new element—flirtation.

Simple flirtation, Trish reminded herself. Common enough, even in the completely, utterly and wholly nonsexual friendship she had with him.

Out of the corner of her eye, she noticed that the waitress was cashing in her tips at the register and the grill man had just brought out the mop and bucket to clean the floors. She stole a glance at her watch.

"Logan, this Cinderella had better get back home," she said, using the excuse to deflect his provocative talk. "Even though Krysia said her husband could watch X-MEN videos until dawn, I'm sure she'd like us to pick up Fritz asap."

He grabbed the check from under the napkin dispenser and recovered her wrap from the coatrack at the end of the counter. As they left the restaurant, he gave the waitress enough money to cover the burgers and allow for a generous tip.

Stepping out onto the deserted sidewalk with him, Trish realized what a mistake it had been not to bring a jacket or coat. Her wrap didn't begin to shake off the chill.

"Might be the first frost of the season tonight," Logan observed, pulling off his suit jacket and wrapping it around her shoulders.

"Thanks for the jacket, I..."

She looked up at him, feeling the strong, protective weight of his hand upon her shoulder. *This is a mistake,* her inner voice warned, as her eyes misted with emotion, as his face neared hers.

The folly was as much her fault as his, because even with the voice of reason telling her no, her heart beat an insistent rhythm that said yes.

Her lips parted lightly as she accepted the gentle touch of his own. She closed her eyes and felt as if she was being lifted to another world.

Even as she wanted him, even as her fingers clung to him, even as she strained to meet him— even then, she felt within her a denying emotion.

A sob escaped her when their lips parted.

"My God, Trish, what's wrong?" Logan

asked, brushing away a tear that had splashed upon her cheek. "Have I done something wrong?"

Trish shook her head.

"Nothing," she admitted. "It's just... It's just...I haven't...I haven't been this close to a man since my husband..."

"Oh, God, I'm so sorry," Logan said, his arms falling to his sides.

He saw things with sudden, blinding clarity.

If he took things any further, he would have to do it for love. He would have to play for keeps. Because Trish couldn't do things any other way.

Even if Fritz weren't in the picture, Trish wasn't the kind of woman for a casual affair.

As the thought of Fritz, that carrot-topped imp, came into his head, Logan pulled away from her, his skin prickling with a sudden chill.

He couldn't hurt that little boy. And it would certainly hurt Fritz to be witness to a romance that was fleeting. Fritz was too young to understand one-night stands, fleeting affairs, casual lovers, and—Logan thought grimly—men who didn't have within them the emotional strength for the sacrifices of a lifetime relationship.

And that was just it. Logan couldn't promise

anything more than something casual, something fleeting, something that would fit in with the real life he lived, the one on the streets, the one in the squad car, the one at the precinct.

He had felt his attraction to the pretty widow increasing for some time; his thoughts had turned to her more frequently than he liked to admit. But he knew his feelings didn't run deep enough for him to give up anything.

His freedom. His work. His world.

She needed security, she needed a "suit." She needed someone who would court her carefully and marry her.

Logan couldn't give her any of that, even though the sweet taste of her lips made him linger, torturing him with proximity to what he couldn't have.

"I shouldn't have done that," Logan said, pulling away even farther from her. "I'm sorry. Your friendship is very important to me."

She looked at him, for all the world as if she had been slapped in the face, and Logan realized just how fragile she was. He felt his anger rise at the thought of any other man kissing her, holding her, possibly hurting her in the ordinary ways that romantic partners do. As he was doing now, without wanting to. Damn. She deserved better than this.

"Not because I didn't want to kiss you," he added. "Not because you're not beautiful and not because you're not a woman I want. But because...well, just because I'm not the kind of man you need. I'm not the kind of man *you* want."

He struggled with his words as she remained silent. He realized he wasn't making sense.

"I'm not the kind of man Fritz needs," he tried again, even though the words tore at his heart. "I'm not the kind of steady, dependable, secure man Fritz needs. I'm better as a friend, Trish. Not as anything more. And I was the one who just breached the boundaries of our friendship. I'm sorry if it made you cry."

That's not what made me cry, Trish thought to herself as they continued to walk down the street, passing the Book Stall and Charles Variety Store in silence.

"I cried because it's been so long since something that deeply emotional has been opened up inside of me," she whispered quietly, so quietly that she was certain he didn't hear her.

Tonight's events—especially Logan's kiss—made her realize something about herself. She had become so focused on Fritz and his well-being at this critical and difficult time in his young life that she hadn't had the inner reserves to give herself the extra care she so desperately needed. Now, to be touched by someone, to be close and vulnerable to someone, rendered her incapable of holding in the swell of emotions.

She wasn't sorry, either, she concluded. At least not now, although she recognized that the tenderness of the evening could very well change in the cold, unforgiving light of morning.

Before she could stop herself, before she could think of all the reasons she should turn away, she drew him near.

"Don't be sorry," she whispered.

As their lips brushed against each other, they both felt a caution—a flashing red light telling them they had every reason to stop, that there was trouble on the tracks ahead.

But the world isn't made for the cautious, and, not daring to let her go for even an instant, Logan pulled her into a doorway, out of the way of the leaves that fluttered and scuttled along the sidewalk.

He kissed her, really kissed her, the way a woman wants to be kissed, the way that makes a woman lose all sense of reason. The way Trish had never before in her life been kissed.

Chapter Ten

"We'd better go," Logan whispered hoarsely, abruptly pulling away. "Michael can only watch X-MEN videos for so long—the Millers are going to wonder what happened to us."

Her face showed her disappointment only fleetingly, but the sight of her thick lashes lowering to avoid his stare seared him as much as any injury he had ever had while on the force.

He had to push her away before he simply yanked her into his arms and kissed her until morning came!

"You're right, we shouldn't be out so late,"

she agreed with a subdued voice and stepped back onto the sidewalk. "I need to get Fritz in bed."

The woman who had been so vulnerable, so fragile and supple in his arms, had disappeared. His hands ached to reach out and rediscover that woman.

But if he did, the stakes would be very high. Too high for him.

And at least one person would be hurt—Trish. The funny thing was, she didn't even know it. At least, he didn't think she did.

"Trish, I didn't mean to..."

"Logan, forget it," she said crisply, beginning to walk toward the street where the Millers lived. "It was just something that happened. I wouldn't want to ruin a good friendship over a little...flirtation."

This didn't sound like Trish—the woman who kept up such a good clip as she led him down the street he had to hurry to catch her, the woman who spoke in such a dismissive tone.

"Trish, I didn't mean that kiss as just a..."

She whirled around to face him, using one hand to hold her luxuriant hair from being buffeted by the wind. It took every bit of his self-control not to reach out to take that hair into his hands, to bury his face in its softness, to fully inhale the light floral smell that had only been hinted at from a distance. But something about her let him know that he should step back, and he did.

"Logan, I'm not some naive young virgin," she said coolly. "I know we're both attracted to each other. But I'm just not ready—and probably never will be ready—for a one-night stand or a brief fling. I can't do it. And not just because of Fritz, but because I'm just not that kind of woman. And you're not the kind of man who can have anything more."

"Trish, I'm not the kind of guy who sleeps around," Logan said defensively.

"No, but are you the kind of guy who's willing to court me and make a commitment to me that would supersede the one you've made to your work? Are you willing to take a nine-to-five job and come home safely on a commuter train in time for dinner every evening? Are you the kind of guy who's going to give me and my son the kind of security we need?"

Logan felt a choking sensation at his neck. Suddenly he couldn't think of the attraction that had been eating away at him for weeks, he couldn't think of the longing that had grown with each passing day. All he could think of was the men who came home to Hubbard Woods on the trains every evening—that wasn't Logan Powell.

He tugged at his tie and felt a spasm of relief as the top button of his collar popped off.

If only he could find emotional peace as easily.

"You're not that kind of guy," Trish answered for him softly. "You're not. And that's okay. We're friends, Logan, great friends, but I can never be your lover. Not for a night, not for a month, not for a year, not even for life—if a life with the police force is the life you have to offer us. I have a boy who depends on me. I can't be selfish."

She was so close and yet so unattainable as she stood near him. If he wanted to, he knew he could take her into his arms and persuade her. She was uncertain, and he suspected that he could change her mind, break down her defenses with another kiss.

But was it worth everything—to exploit her vulnerability, her needs that she was only dimly aware of?

God, just one more kiss, he thought, feeling like a heel because he knew that there was a part

of him that wanted, needed, to bruise her lips
with his and the heartache be damned.

Just…one…more…kiss.

She touched his lips with her fingers, stopping
him.

"No, Logan," she begged. "Please don't."

And then he realized that he had spoken aloud
his most private wish to kiss her and kiss her
again. Looking at her, he also realized that her
emotions were laid bare so completely that she
ached for him to take advantage of her, even if
she didn't know that she felt that longing so
deeply.

He could take advantage of her for the night.

And know he had betrayed her.… He couldn't
do it.

"All right, stop tempting me," he growled
with mock sternness.

He took her arm in his, ignoring the electric
sensations which passed between them. If he
was going to be a friend, he was going to have
to act like one, he thought to himself.

They hurried up the block to the Miller house.
Although Krysia had already gone to bed, Michael Miller was still up—which Trish was
grateful for. At least Michael didn't notice the
guilty traces of her lipstick on Logan's lip as

Krysia would have done. He simply led them into the living room, where Paul and Fritz lay on top of bean bag chairs in front of the television.

Logan gently picked up Fritz and cradled him in his arms with a fierce protectiveness. The sight made Trish fill with longing and with an even greater determination to resist any urges she might have to reconsider her attraction to Logan.

Fritz would need a man in his life. At that last thought, she bit her lip.

That man wouldn't, *couldn't* be Logan Powell.

They walked back to the apartment, and as they walked in silence, Trish felt a sense of loss that reminded her of the more profound loss she had felt at her husband's death. So close to an emotional connection with the man next to her, who carried her son so tenderly, and yet— That closeness had brought her face to face with just how much emptiness there was in her life.

Without question, tonight had made her see that she needed to pay more attention to her own needs. And yet, it was ironic that the man who had made her see her own vulnerabilities wasn't

the man who could help her with those vulnerabilities—to open up, to love and be loved.

"I'll give you a call over the weekend," Logan said, after he laid Fritz on his bed and
helped Trish with taking off the boy's shoes and
putting the blanket over him. "Fritz has been
bugging me about that dinner we never had at
Felicia's."

"Oh, it's those paper fans that come with the
drinks," Trish said lightly. She congratulated
herself on her casual tone. She was beginning to
feel some of her equilibrium returning.

Obviously the kiss they'd shared hadn't been
as profoundly disturbing and disorienting and
discombobulating to Logan as it had been to her,
so she worked to avoid some of the embarrass-
ment of having her emotions laid bare by af-
fecting his nonchalance. He had bounced back
very nicely from their kiss.

She could, too.

"Maybe we could take him to Felicia's one
night after karate class," Logan whispered.
"That's a great kid you have there."

"I know," Trish said, wondering if even having dinner together as friends would be a bad
idea for her son.

He would be disappointed when Logan moved

back to the city, back to his real life. Even though Fritz knew that Logan would be going sometime...

But then, looking at her boy sleeping peacefully, she decided she was wrong. Fritz already had enough invested into the relationship with Logan. To cut it off now would be wrong. When Logan moved, there would simply be a gradual wearing away of the emotional connection. She was sure that Logan could be persuaded to occasionally come up for a dinner or a lunch at McDonald's, and those meetings would simply come farther and farther apart as Logan's life grew busier and busier.

"He really has gotten a lot out of his relationship with you," Trish said as they moved out of the room and headed for the front door of the apartment. "I'm grateful to you."

"Grateful," Logan repeated in a voice still barely above a whisper. Why did that hurt so much?

After a somewhat awkward goodbye, he walked down the narrow, steep stairs to the street. As he put the small apartment further behind him, he felt himself gaining speed, until, as his feet hit the sidewalk, he found himself breaking out into a run.

He hadn't felt the wind at his heels like this since the shooting. The doctors had warned him against straining the internal stitches. And yet, now, as he raced the wind, beating an invisible opponent, he didn't care what damage he might do to his body. He sprinted down Chestnut street, turning down Elm and then gathering even more energy as he raced for the lake.

Nothing could catch him, he thought to himself as he ran.

He was as fast as he had been when he was a youngster in training for his black belt, as quick as the cop he had been.

And yet, as he got within a block of the beach, he felt a cramp on his arm where he had been knifed three years before, he felt a little twinge on his leg where it had been broken during a footrace with a criminal, and, with the dark water in sight, he felt his stomach muscles clench in protest against his newest injury.

No, he corrected himself grimly. His newest injury was the one inside his head, he had to admit as he flung himself onto the nearest pine bench on the sand.

The next morning, he wasn't surprised when he got a phone call from his commanding officer, Gary Lawson.

"Logan, we've missed you," Gary said. "I looked on the disabled list, and I see your time's up. Come on back—we need you and, knowing you, I'll bet you've been spending the past few months counting the days."

"How would you know that?" Logan asked. Frankly, he *hadn't* been counting the days. At least not in the past few weeks.

"Oh, you're just like me. Career guy. Nothing'll ever take you off the force," Gary said. "So, I'll be seeing you week from Thursday— 0800. And make some time for us to have a cup of coffee that day so I can catch you up on everything."

"Give me a hint. What's been happening?" Logan asked, thankful that the old instinct was kicking in. He was starting to look forward again to the world he had left behind.

"Same stuff, different day. You know it never changes."

"Right," Logan agreed. "I'll see you then."

As he put the phone back on the receiver, he looked around the house. He had grown up here—had sat in this very chair when he'd studied during high school, had carved the initials

LP on the underside of its wooden arms. As he got up and made a cup of coffee, he studied the house. And was reminded at every turn of the family life that had come before.

This was the kitchen table where his family had eaten nearly every meal—he could almost taste the macaroni and cheese, smothered with the ketchup that he and Bill had insisted on adding to his mother's recipe. This was the living room couch on which he had waited for his brother to come home, long after his curfew, always with some excuse. Here were the marks that he and his brother had put on the doorjamb to the den, with dates and initials to commemorate their growth. Logan rubbed the penciled marks with his finger until the growth spurt he and Bill had had in junior high school was rubbed out.

It was a house with memories and perhaps it was a good thing that he planned to sell it. No need to keep a home that was his only connection to his brother. No need to have a houseful of memories in the suburbs when he was working in the city, even if the department wasn't ruled by the city ordinance that required its officers to live inside the city limits. His city apartment was clear of memories, a simple box for a simple man.

He paused as he looked out onto the front yard. It was where his father had played football with the two brothers, patiently shepherding them from awkward toddlers to talented teens. Logan could almost see himself racing across the lawn, a football cradled in one arm, and Bill with his hands outstretched for the tackle.

And with that memory, he was reminded of another boy.

A boy who deserved to have the chance to run breathlessly with the ball, outracing the tackle, lunging for the end zone.

A boy whose mother deserved the best that a man could give.

Chapter Eleven

Logan tried telephoning Trish's apartment, but no one answered. Feeling an unbearable restlessness, he wanted to share his news and the only person he could think of as important enough in his life was her. He didn't leave a message on her machine.

He would find her. He had to find her, because his news was meaningless without Trish.

He walked over to the pharmacy, but when he rang up the security buzzer at her apartment, there was no response.

He was surprised that, even as important as the news was, he didn't want to call or see anyone but her. He didn't want to go out with his buddies from the precinct to celebrate, the way he had when he had come back from leaves before.

The desire to find her, to talk to her, grew in direct proportion to his frustration that he could not. And the intensity of his feelings surprised him. How had she become so important to him so quickly? How had she become so much a part of what made his life meaningful?

He shoved aside the question of what he would do when he returned to the police department—with whom he would share his successes and his failures, with whom he would spend his time. Who would he call his best friend?

He stepped into Charles Variety Store on the off chance that she was shopping with Fritz.

He asked the clerk at the Book Stall because Trish said she often picked up a paperback there. But no one had seen her this day.

It wasn't until he reached the library that he remembered where she might be.

She spent Wednesday afternoons with Fritz at the park two blocks from the apartment above the pharmacy. It was good, she said, for Fritz to get out. To be outside. To run free.

It was a chilly, overcast day and the park was almost empty. Logan felt his heart beat more rapidly as he recognized the two figures at the baseball diamond. Trish was using the solitude to teach Fritz how to play baseball, pitching to him and cheering his batting practice.

As Logan came up from the grassy outfield, Trish pitched again.

"Strike three!" Fritz howled. "That's strike three and I'm out. I'm no good at baseball!"

"No, that pitch didn't count. Let's try again," Trish urged. "You'll get the hang of it! Just keep your eyes on the ball."

She pitched again, an unbearably slow underhand throw that arced right into Fritz's upheld bat. Logan heard the crack of the ball hitting wood.

"Yeah!" Trish shouted.

The ball flew high and long. As it sped toward Logan, Fritz shouted a hello. Trish acknowledged him, and as she turned her attention back to Fritz, Logan tried to persuade himself that there wasn't the slightest reservation in her attitude toward him.

"Run! Run, Fritz! Run!" Trish screamed. "Get to first base!"

Fritz, momentarily confused but a quick

learner, dropped his bat and headed down the baseline toward first. Trish came up behind him, and held up a gloved hand for the ball. Logan caught it and threw. She could have easily tagged Fritz out, but she didn't.

"Great job, Fritz!" She exclaimed. "You beat me. Wow! I almost had you, but you're safe."

"Way to go!" Logan added, trotting easily up to the base. "Does Mom bat now, or me?"

"Neither," Trish admitted, pointing across the field to the parking lot. A van had arrived, bearing uniformed Little Leaguers. "Come on, Fritz, time to give up the field."

"Aw, Mom," Fritz complained. "I wish we had our own yard to play in and we didn't have to share with everyone."

"Well, we do have to share," she said. "How 'bout a walk?"

"Can I join you?" Logan asked. "I have some news I wanted to tell you."

"What is it?" Fritz asked, joining them. "Is it good news or bad news?"

"Good news," Logan said, but as soon as he said it, he realized that it might not end up seeming like good news. Would she be happy for him? Would she miss him? Would he be as happy to be leaving as he'd thought he might be?

"Well, how 'bout the Sweet Shoppe?" Fritz asked. "That's where I like to celebrate good news."

He looked up at his mother beseechingly, and Trish laughed.

"All right, if you promise to eat every bite of your dinner."

They headed across the street in silence, Logan trying to formulate how he would tell them that he was going back to Chicago. He'd looked forward to the day when his commander would call him back. He had waited impatiently, never considering that he might not be so excited once he was taken off the disabled list.

Yet, looking at Trish, he really didn't know how she would feel with the news that he was leaving. She might be glad to have him out of her life.

Maybe he was just another complication for her, one that she would be happy to forgo. He couldn't offer her the things she needed—and she might not have room in her life, in her heart, for a man like him. Maybe she looked forward to his going with relief.

On the other hand, maybe she would miss

him. And while the idea of Trish missing him was something that filled him with a bittersweet pride, he knew it wasn't a feeling that he fully relished.

At the Sweet Shoppe, Logan bought himself and Trish diet colas and a quarter pound of candy for Fritz.

"Thanks," Fritz said as they sat down at the ornate iron chairs and diminutive marble-topped table.

"So, what's your news?" Trish asked.

Logan hesitated, suddenly hearing a warning voice in his head that told him this wasn't the way to handle things. He should tell Trish first, on her own, in order to give them both a chance to prepare Fritz. Yet, his going back to work couldn't possibly affect Fritz that much, could it?

"I've been called back," he said simply. "I'm going back to work Thursday."

As soon as the words were out of his mouth, he regretted them. Fritz looked stricken. Trish's attention was focused on her son, gauging his reactions.

"You're leaving us?" Fritz choked.

"I'm not leaving you," Logan explained.

"I've been called back to work. We've talked about this, tiger. I'm a cop and that's my..."

"Don't call me tiger."

Logan took a deep breath. This conversation wasn't going anything like he expected. Why was Fritz taking it so hard? Fritz had his mother, he had his friends, and he would always have Logan as a friend....

"I'm going back to work as a detective in the city," he said. "That's what I've always done. I don't know how to do anything else."

"Will you ever come back?" Fritz asked, his voice taking on a thin, desperate quality.

"Of course," Logan said, even as he wondered if he was lying. "I can come back maybe even every week to see you and your mom."

"No, I mean, are you going to be coming back every night to live here?" Fritz persisted.

"I'm afraid not," Logan said, feeling lower than a snake as he watched the feelings of betrayal and sadness in Fritz's eyes.

"You'll be in the city all the time," Fritz said dismally. "You're leaving us."

"It's not like that."

"It sure is."

"We should be happy for Logan," Trish said

quickly, shooting Logan a look that confirmed she thought he was the equivalent of a pit viper.

"Trish, I should have told you first...." he said lamely.

"Mom, he's *leaving* us."

"This is what he has to do, Fritz, he's a detective and he can't really do his work here in Hubbard Woods."

Fritz's paper bag of candy dropped to the floor.

Logan reached down to pick it up. As he looked at Fritz, he saw that the boy was crying.

"Oh, Fritz, I don't mean to hurt..."

"God Damned You!" Fritz screamed.

The two women standing at the counter stopped their conversation to stare. The counterman poked his head out the door from the back room.

"Fritz," Trish said soothingly, putting an arm around his shoulder. "It's all right...."

He threw off his mother's arm, and ran for the door.

Logan grabbed him before he could make it.

"Come on, Fritz, I'm sorry, I—"

Fritz struggled in his arms, his tiny fists flailing at Logan. The little boy struggled as Logan tightened his grip. To his face and arms Fritz's punches were like pelts of rain and hail in a summer storm. To his heart, though, they felt like hammer blows. At last, Fritz dissolved into racking sobs.

"Dear God, I had no idea," Logan said to Trish as she pulled her son, limp and without protest, from his arms. "Trish, I can see now that I should have told you first. To help prepare him for this. I never thought it would be such a big deal with him. I thought he knew I had to go back."

"Logan, he loves you so much," she said quietly, barely audible over Fritz's crying. "I better take him home."

She walked toward the door, and as Logan watched them leave, he felt an unbearable sadness—as near to complete abandonment as he'd ever felt.

Would it end like this? he wondered.

"What about you?" he called after her.

But she was already heading down the sidewalk, and Logan couldn't bring himself to follow her. If he did, he knew he would never be able to walk away again.

And he knew that the department needed him. He had heard the anxiety in Gary's voice. It wasn't anything new, it wasn't anything that wouldn't be there next week, next month, next year, but the police department needed him.

And he needed his work. He needed it to fight back at the demons within him, the ones that told him he wasn't good enough, that he needed to do penance.

He couldn't walk away from the force.

He didn't have any choice, even if the days when police work had been fresh and energetic and positive for him were long since over.

So it had to end. Just like this.

He threw down a tip for the waitress, gulped at the cool diet cola, and headed for home.

Trish carried Fritz up the stairs to their apartment and put him on her lap as she sank onto the living room couch. His sobs had quieted and now he was simply limp with grief. She kissed his forehead and brushed his hair back from his face.

"I don't want to take karate anymore," Fritz said. "It's a stupid class, anyhow."

"Fritz, you can't quit everything just because you're hurt," she said.

"I'm not talking about quitting everything," Fritz cried. "I just want to quit *karate*. I don't want to see him anymore."

Trish closed her eyes, wondering what she could say.

Although she knew that Logan hadn't meant to cause any pain to Fritz and herself, she wished that things could have been different. It was her fault as much as Logan's, because she should have seen Fritz's adoration of Logan and recognized the possibilities. A little boy could so easily read betrayal in something as simple as Logan going back to the rest of his life.

"How about if we see how you feel later?" she said, knowing that the hurt she felt about Logan leaving rendered her powerless to say the things she should say.

He'll still see you. He cares for you very much. We'll go into the city sometimes to see him.

She couldn't speak. So she sat, brushing away his tears when he cried and listening to his petal-soft snores when he fell into an exhausted sleep. When he awoke, she suggested a game of X-MEN action figures.

A half hour later, she left a subdued Fritz playing with his toys in his bedroom while she tried to concentrate on what to make for dinner. When the phone rang, she wasn't surprised that it was Logan.

If she had any anger at Logan for having mishandled telling Fritz about his return to work, it was gone as soon as she heard the concern in his voice.

"How's Fritz?"

"Better," Trish admitted. "But he's still pretty upset."

"Would it help if I came over? Or maybe if I saw him later?"

Trish thought about the little boy who had lashed out so violently at the betrayal by his hero.

"Give it some time," she said. "I don't know what to do. But I think he feels very intensely about this and I think that it's too explosive to confront those feelings right now."

"Well, when you think he's ready, I'll be here," Logan said. "I just didn't realize how important this might be to him."

"I know."

"Trish, there's something else we didn't have a chance to talk about."

"What?" she asked, with a sense of foreboding.

"How do you feel about my going back?"

She paused, biting her lip hard.

"I feel very happy for you," she said cautiously. "Going back to the force is something you've really looked forward to. And you're so good at what you do that I know you're very much needed."

"I'm not asking any of that. I want to know— are you going to miss me?" he asked. The crackle of the telephone line filled the uncomfortable pause. "Or is that an unfair question?"

"That's an unfair question," she said, knowing that she didn't have the courage to lay her emotions out on the table when his own feelings were so clearly of a more casual, less intense variety. "But, of course, I'll miss you," she added with admirable ease. "You've been very good to Fritz."

The last was a very safe response, one that squarely put their relationship back on the solid footing of focusing on Fritz. After all, this friendship had begun with Fritz's karate lessons.

"I'll miss you, too," Logan said softly.

Trish didn't say anything. She didn't know how to measure the meaning of his words.

The silence stretched uncomfortably.

"So I should wait for you to tell me that I can see Fritz?" Logan asked.

"I think that would be a wise idea."

"Then I'll be waiting."

They said their goodbyes with an awkward straddling of the casual assumption that, as friends, they would see each other quite soon but with the difficult truth that, as friends, they were now parting in a very subtle, yet definite way.

Chapter Twelve

"I'm here for only one reason," Logan said sternly as his brother sat down across from him and put the telephone to his ear.

"Whatever it is, I'm just glad to see you," Bill said.

Logan grimaced.

This visit might turn out to be harder than he'd thought. He studied his brother for the first time in three years.

Where was the brother with the devil-may-care swagger? Where was the brother who could lie, cheat, steal with his smug, superior smile never leaving his face? Where was the brother who had made fun of Logan for being on the straight and narrow?

This man—this impostor—who sat across from him in the visiting room of the Stateville Prison couldn't possibly be the Bill Powell he had grown up with.

Softer around the edges, a little bit of gray around the temples, wearing the blue jumpsuit of all prisoners, Bill had a more peaceful, contented look to him. The barefaced hostility of his twenties was gone.

Logan had seen men worn down by prison, but those men harbored the broken quality that was absent in the man seated before him. It was almost as if prison agreed with Bill.

"I've missed you," Bill said. "And I have a lot of things to tell you—the first of which is that I'm sorry."

"Don't start with me," Logan warned.

For a split second, he had trusted his brother's words. But then, Logan remembered the many cons Bill had pulled—all starting with seeming repentance for the last con.

"You have every reason to mistrust me," Bill admitted. "I've certainly done everything I could in my life to destroy any brotherly love you may have had when I was born. But I'm a changed man, Logan. I really am.''

''Let's just stick to the reason why I came here,'' Logan said.

''All right,'' Bill acquiesced. ''What brings you here to see me?''

''The house,'' Logan said. ''When our parents died, they left everything to both of us, including the house. I know the usual thing to do is to sell it and split the proceeds but I'd like simply to buy you out.''

''You're going to live there?''

''That's none of your business,'' Logan shot back, and then relented. ''No, I'm not going to live there. I'd like to give the house to a friend.''

Bill whistled softly. ''Must be a good friend.''

''Yes, he is.''

Bill raised an eyebrow.

''He's five years old,'' Logan explained, feeling irritated that he was getting off track. ''I want to make a gift of the house to him and his mother. So I've come to talk about buying you out.''

''You can't,'' Bill said.

Damn! Logan thought to himself.

He never should have come here. His hands itched to simply slam the receiver down and walk out. His brother was going to make this as tough as—

"You can't buy me out because I'll just give my half of the house to you," Bill explained. "You see, I know that you were paying the mortgage for our parents toward the end, when they were both sick. Mom wrote to me about it. I think of it as really your house already."

Logan's eyes narrowed.

"All right, Bill, out with it. What have you got hidden up your sleeve? What's the catch?"

"Nothing. I swear it. But what I do have is an apology. One that you've deserved for a long time. I've acted like a jerk all my life. But, Logan, I'm a different man now. I've done a lot of thinking since I got here—and I realized that I can go in two different directions when I leave this place. If I blame others for my problems and keep a chip on my shoulder, I can go in one direction. If I take responsibility for everything I've done, I can get on with my life. I can be a changed man. I can start over."

"Is this the prologue to a demand for money?"

"Not at all," Bill protested. "I'm making my apologies to you, apologies that I wrote to you at a time last year when you weren't ready to read my letters."

"Those letters," Logan murmured. "I returned them."

"Yeah," Bill said. "And I guess that if I were in your shoes, I probably would have done the same thing."

"What did they say?"

"They said that I loved you. And that I was sorry. And that I hoped that we could be brothers, real brothers, from now on."

"It sounds very pat," Logan said warily.

"I'm prepared to accept the fact that you don't believe me," Bill said amiably.

"About the house…"

"I'm telling you that if you want to turn over the house to a friend, I won't even ask all the questions that natural curiosity demands. The house is yours to do with as you want."

"And what do you want in return?" Logan challenged.

"Forgiveness."

Logan felt as if he had been punched in the stomach.

He looked at his brother, searching for the con artist he had grown—if he was honest—to hate. The same smile was there. The one that had charmed his mother so many times, robbed hometown girls of their virtue and scammed total strangers of their cash. Bill still had the same disarming way of pushing his hair back from his forehead. Bill still looked at him with beguiling eyes that could turn to tears when it would help his cause.

And yet, wasn't there something different about his younger brother?

"Forgiveness, brother," Bill repeated.

After a moment's hesitation, Logan slammed the telephone receiver down and stood up, not caring when his chair fell backward.

He stumbled down the aisle of visiting booths, throwing a brusque, "Excuse me," behind him when he jostled a woman standing by the wall, heading blindly for the door.

Damn him, damn him, damn him, Logan thought, feeling the explosion of fury at Bill which had so often propelled him to action.

He shouldn't have come here. He should have taken care of the matter of the house through lawyers. Shouldn't have left himself so vulnerable to the feelings of love and hurt and betrayal and anger and guilt.

Why had he decided to deal with the house himself, face-to-face with Bill?

At the thought of his parents' house, he thought again of Trish. He was doing this for her. He had changed his mind, turning away from cynical thoughts about Bill, in order to give her a chance. Look where that had gotten him.

The question was, with the image of her soft and gentle face in his mind, could he turn back?

He stood at the door, ramming his fist against the doorjamb until his knuckles bled.

And then, exhausted, he headed back.

When he reached the visitors' carrel, his brother sat where he had left him. Bill's head was down, his shoulders convulsing with sobs, the telephone still held in his hand.

Logan knocked on the glass that separated them.

Bill looked up, his eyes filled with tears.

Logan picked up the receiver.

"Forgiven," he said softly, and held his palm against the glass.

As his brother placed his palm on the other side of the glass, Logan realized it was the closest they would get to hugging each other. It still felt good.

"You told me I didn't have to go," Fritz complained, not even looking up from a favorite cartoon.

"I let you get out of going on Tuesday, but I think you should at least try to go today."

"Paul's not going."

"Paul's got chicken pox. He doesn't have to go."

"I wish I had chicken pox."

Trish watched her son's face as the flickering light from the television played upon his impassive features. She impulsively switched off the set.

He looked up at her with a stare that was one part surprise, two parts unhappiness and five parts just plain stubbornness.

"What did you do that for?" he asked.

"Because you've been watching television nonstop today. And yesterday. And the day before yesterday. Every time I've told you to stop, you've stopped...but only until my back is turned."

"So?" He regarded her coolly.

And suddenly Trish longed for her son, the real one who had emotions, even if they were negative, and not the Fritz who sat in front of her now, the one who seemed to have lost the ability to feel.

Since Logan had said he was going back on the force, Fritz had become a different kid.

That five parts of stubbornness hadn't been part of his makeup before.

"Come on, we're going," she ordered.

"Where?"

"Karate class."

"No way."

"*Yes* way," she said, even though she felt about as inclined to go as he did. It would be so much easier to just let it go, let him watch his cartoons, let her tackle the pile of paperwork on the dining room table.

"But Logan's gone," Fritz whined.

"That's right, he is," she said sternly. "He's going to work in the city and he will only be able to see us as his schedule permits."

"Then I feel too upset to go to karate," Fritz said. "Besides, it's a stupid class."

"I didn't hear you say it was a stupid class when you were trying your best," Trish said.

"I'm still upset."

"As for being upset, don't you think I'm upset, too?" she blurted out.

"You never look like you're upset," Fritz pointed out.

"Well, I am," she admitted. "But I know this

is important to Logan and, if you really care about him, you have to be willing to let him do what he really wants to do and still be his friend. It's like Mommy—when you grow up, you may end up going away to another city, maybe even another state, to go to college. I'll miss you, but because I love you so much, I'll be happy that you're doing what you want to do. I'm still going to love you, wherever you live, whatever you do."

She studied her son, knowing that—at this moment—she, too, was learning a lesson about love.

If she really cared about Logan, she would have to be willing to let him follow his destiny, to do what it was that he wanted. If she wanted to be a friend, a good friend, to him, she had to love him—regardless of whether he was in the city or in Hubbard Woods, whether he was wearing a suit and tie or wearing a policeman's badge.

Fritz came to her and put his arms around her neck.

"Mommy, I told you before," he said. "I'm going to buy you a nice house here in Hubbard Woods when I grow up. And we'll live in it together and it will have a big backyard for playing.''

She held on to his hug for just an instant longer than he wanted. ''I love you,'' she said as he squirmed out of her arms.

''I love you, too, Mommy,'' Fritz said. ''Did you wash my *gi?*''

Trish smiled, her heart overflowing with love for her son. ''Yes, it's in your closet. Get changed quickly—if we hurry, we'll just be able to make the beginning of class.''

As Fritz changed into his karate uniform, Trish ran a comb through her tousled hair and looked for her purse. She felt lighter, freed somehow from the heavy weight of emotion that had been pressing against her chest for the past few days.

She could be a friend to Logan, a good one, in fact. But she would have to let him do what he was best at—being a police officer. She would have to be his friend even if it meant that he lived in another city, faced danger every day of the week, and even if someday that friendship would end with her having to explain to Fritz about another death. She could do all those things, safe in the knowledge that Logan was doing what made him the happiest. Because he would never be happy staying in Hubbard Woods. Or would he?

She thought of him at the park, pushing Fritz on the swing and chasing him through the jungle gym. He had seemed happy. She remembered him on long walks, relaxed and smiling as they passed through the residential and shop-lined streets. He had seemed happy.

But he had always talked of going back, a voice reminded her, and, besides, his sense of guilt and shame about his brother would keep him on the force long after any happiness with the actual job was over.

As a friend, I can support him, Trish thought, stiffening her spine. And I can teach my son to support him.

But as a lover? her inner voice asked as she stopped in front of the bathroom mirror to check her appearance.

She wiped vigorously at an ink mark on her cheek and opened the medicine cabinet to find some lipstick to counteract the pallor that had come over her face.

A lover?

She stared at herself, evaluating the image that she had been far too busy to confront.

He didn't ask me to be a lover, she reminded

herself, thinking back to their kisses. He had been the one to apologize, no doubt knowing that he couldn't offer her the same feelings that a lover would offer. For a night, for a brief affair, for the rest of his life. And he must have realized that to take advantage of her willingness when there was a little boy to consider would have been wrong.

He didn't have romantic feelings for her.

Did she have those feelings for him?

"I plead the fifth," she joked out loud to her mirror image. "On the grounds that it might incriminate me, I refuse to answer the question."

"Who are you talking to, Mom?" Fritz asked.

Trish whirled around and gazed with pleasure at her son, forgetting her own ambivalent feelings.

"Come here, you," she commanded, holding out her arms for another hug.

In a few more years, she knew, those hugs would be few and far between as he would be too cool, too old, too hip to hug his mother willingly.

As they embraced, she felt grateful for God's gift of Fritz Eastman. Even if he made her life infinitely more complicated, she would never have it any other way.

"Let's get going," she said huskily, letting him slip from her arms.

Hand in hand, they walked to the car. Quickly she drove the three blocks to the Community House. At the door of the gym, several moms and sons stood in a small knot.

"What's going on?" Trish asked.

"No class today," a mother said, gesturing to a piece of paper that had been taped to the closed door.

Trish stepped closer.

Karate Classes Canceled Until Further Notice.

She felt a shudder pass through her.

"My neighbor called me this morning and said it was a gang ambush," one mother said. "It's such a shame—he was such a young man and he did so much for the community."

"I heard a rumor it was a drug bust that went awry," another said. "Either way, he was a wonderful karate teacher."

I don't like the way these women use the past tense, Trish thought, as she felt her mouth go dry.

"What are you talking about?" she asked finally.

"The reason the class is canceled," the first

mother explained. "Logan Powell got shot. He's in the hospital. Didn't you hear?"

Trish looked at her son Fritz, and saw his mouth open into a small, perfectly round O. She grabbed his hand and was halfway down the hall toward the front desk before she called back a goodbye to the mothers.

"What happened to Logan?" Fritz asked.

"I don't know."

"Is he dead?"

"I don't know."

"Were there bad guys?"

"I don't know."

At the front desk, she asked the receptionist what had happened to Logan Powell.

"I just got on duty twenty minutes ago," the receptionist said. "So don't ask me. All I know is that he's at Sacred Heart Hospital."

"Where's that?"

"Go down Sheridan Road. It's right on the border of Chicago and Hubbard Woods."

Trish grabbed Fritz's hand and together they ran to the parking lot.

Chapter Thirteen

As she drove, Trish wondered if she was ready to bear another death. She glanced briefly at her son in the passenger seat next to her, and wondered if he was ready.

It wouldn't come to that, she thought, feverishly, raising up another prayer for Logan's safety.

This is what it will be like to be Logan's friend, to be Logan's lover, she thought to herself. Frantic trips to hospitals, uncertainty at every turn, a repetition of the night that turned her from a wife into a widow.

Was it all worth it?

She softened the pressure on the accelerator as she realized she was edging ten miles over the speed limit.

She thought of the man who had set limits on her son, who had had the courage to discipline him when others might have been too soft. She thought of the man who had set free her son's emotions, who had given him confidence and a sense of importance with his tutoring. She thought of the man who had befriended her son with little to gain for himself. And she thought of the man who had opened up a door to her own feelings, a door that she thought had been slammed shut forever.

She pulled into the Sacred Heart Hospital emergency room entrance, and searched frantically for a parking place.

"It's okay, Mom," Fritz said. "No matter what's happened to him, it's okay."

Trish wasn't sure she believed her son, but she admired the courage he was showing. She breathed deeply, calming herself, and pulled into a space.

"All right, let's go," she said, jumping out of the car.

"Mom, you forgot something," Fritz said, coming up behind her and taking her hand. "The rule you always taught me was that you have to hold hands when you cross a parking lot or a street. What am I going to do with you?''

She smiled at her son's use of her own frequent lament and squeezed his hand. They walked briskly to the emergency room entrance, found the front desk and waited until a nurse was free before asking for Logan.

''He's still here in the emergency room and he's fine,'' the nurse said. ''But our rules are that only his family can be admitted to see him. He's scheduled to be released in a few hours. You can wait for him over there in the waiting room.''

Trish breathed a sigh of relief at the nurse's words. Logan was okay. He was going to be released. She wondered if they should just stay in the waiting room, because she knew Logan didn't have any family to be with him....

''But we are his family,'' Fritz said abruptly. ''I'm his son. This is his wife.''

Trish gave him a stern look. How could he lie...?

''Fine, your mommy can go on in, but young boys can't go into the emergency room,'' the nurse admonished Fritz.

''You wouldn't want me to stay all by myself

in the lobby here, would you?'' Fritz asked slyly. "When I'm by myself, I can be a lot of trouble. And besides, what happens if a stranger talks to me?''

The nurse regarded him coolly for a split second.

"All right, both of you, get in there. Your husband's in bed fourteen, Mrs. Powell.''

Before Trish could say a word, Fritz grabbed her hand and tugged.

"Come on, Mrs. Powell,'' he ordered with an authority that few five-year-olds possess.

As she followed him past the iron doors, she squeezed his hand in warning.

"Fritz, where did you ever learn to lie like that?''

"I saw it on television,'' he said. "It worked, didn't it?''

"I suppose,'' Trish said. "But remind me to cut your television time.''

They filed past thirteen beds in the emergency room, and as she'd seen the progressive medical dramas, Trish wondered if it was such a good idea for Fritz to come with her. But he walked with such confidence that Trish didn't have the heart to order him to stay in the lobby.

At bed fourteen, she pulled away the curtain.

She followed Fritz and entered a tiny cubicle. Logan lay in a bed, his right arm in a cast and his forehead bandaged, his face unnaturally pale. Trish gasped, feeling intense sympathetic pains in her own body. Logan looked up and smiled a smile that made everything—the trip, the anxiety, her own son lying—worth it.

As their eyes met, they communicated to each other the joy and delight of being together again.

"My God, Trish, come here," he whispered, holding out his good hand to her.

She couldn't have stopped herself. Throwing away every ounce of reason and restraint, she rushed forward.

"Darling," he murmured reverently as she sat on the edge of his bed.

He pulled her to his chest, luxuriating in the texture of her hair as he held her to him. She looked up, and he thought she might pull away, but instead, she searched his eyes, as if looking for a lover's reassurance.

He couldn't resist—his lips sought hers. As they met, Logan felt the spark of electricity arcing through him.

They were discovering each other, casting off reservations and replacing trepidation with lovers' courage. Sighing softly, her lips parted as his tongue sought to explore her mouth.

As if from a distance, Logan heard Fritz's voice.

"Oh, gross," the boy said. "If I had known you were going to make kissy-faces, I would have stayed in the waiting room."

Trish jerked away from Logan's embrace. The words of her son brought her back to the reality, the impossibility, of their relationship.

Logan held fast to her hands, unwilling to let her completely escape his embrace.

"How did you find me?" he asked.

She shook her head, momentarily too flustered by their kiss to talk.

"We found out at karate," Fritz explained.

Logan tousled Fritz's hair with his good hand.

"I've never been so happy to see two people in my entire life," he said.

The curtain behind Trish ripped open and a stern-faced nurse entered the cubicle. Guiltily, Trish stood up. In a flash, she thought the receptionist might have discovered that she really wasn't Mrs. Powell and had sent the nurse to throw her out.

"Mrs. Powell," the nurse said, handing her a

sheaf of papers. "Here's the instructions on how to care for Mr. Powell once you get home."

"Mrs. Powell? I kind of like the sound of that," Logan mused, ignoring Trish's sharp glance.

"And Mrs. Powell, could we get you to sign right here, saying that you'll be responsible for his care?" the nurse said, handing her a clipboard.

The guilt about lying, or at least her son lying, was too much for Trish.

"I'm not really Mrs. Powell. I'm just Trish Eastman. And while I'm happy to be responsible for Logan's care, I have to tell you the truth that—"

The nurse looked at her impassively.

"You know these modern women," Fritz piped in. "Won't take her husband's name."

"Whatever your name is, just sign," the nurse said impatiently. "We're a little shorthanded here this afternoon, and I don't have time for a full explanation."

Trish signed on the dotted line and the nurse left.

"All right, so I'm in charge of making sure you get better," Trish said. "So you'll have to do what I tell you to do."

"Gladly."

She ignored his flirtatious tone.

"How did it happen?" Fritz asked. "Were they really bad guys? Did you shoot them back or did you punch them?"

"And how did you manage to get injured your first day back on the job?" Trish demanded.

Logan shrugged.

"Just lucky, I guess, *Mrs. Powell.*"

"That's not my name," Trish corrected.

"Would you change your name if I asked?"

Trish backed away from the bed, seeing the bantering had far too heavy an undercurrent to it.

"You're serious, aren't you? Because you can't joke about something so important in front of Fritz. In front of me, for that matter."

"I'm not joking. Would you have me? I mean, I realized how important you are to me. How much I love you, how much I want to share my life with you."

Trish looked at him, feeling the world of possibilities, lovers' possibilities, opening up for her. As he said the words of love, she knew her feelings were the same, though she'd kept them hidden even from her own self.

Yet, she hesitated. Could she be a policeman's

wife? Could she sit by the phone each day and night he worked, waiting for the call that every policeman's wife dreads? Could she stand the danger, the obsession, the threats?

What was the alternative? Isolation? Never having Logan's arms wrapping around her with love and support?

Yes, she thought to herself, *say yes.*

And then she looked into his eyes, so earnest, so eager as he waited for her to give him the ultimate assurance that a woman can give of her love. Just about to give him her answer, a man's voice interrupted their silent tableau.

"Hi, I'm Dr. Sugarman. And you are...?"

Trish looked over to the foot of the bed, where a middle-aged doctor stood puzzling over a medical file.

"Logan Powell," Logan supplied.

"And Mrs. Powell," Trish added, savoring the smile of relief and love that came over Logan's face.

"So, you were injured in the line of duty," the doctor said, leafing through his file. "Boy, it sounds really vicious."

Trish felt a tremor of fear course through her as she thought of how Logan had been hurt.

"It *was* vicious, Doc," Logan said.

"Your assailant was twelve?" the doctor asked.

"He was in the Intermediate Karate section," Logan supplied, studiously ignoring Trish's look of shock.

"You got injured in karate…?" Trish asked.

"Yes, darling, the kid was doing the crane kick and got me fair and square," Logan said with an infuriatingly smug smile. "Will you still marry me even if I'm not a police hero?"

Trish looked up at the ceiling and counted to ten.

"Of course, she will," Fritz piped in. "But I think you might need to take some more karate lessons."

The wedding was nothing like her first, which had been an extravagant affair with white lace and bridesmaids and rice. Instead, six weeks after his hospital stay, Logan had met Fritz and Trish at the Hubbard Woods Clerk's office and within a half hour, they were a family. It might not have had a lot of pomp and splendor, the bridal party might have worn jeans and Fritz may have been the only attendant, but it was no less moving.

And Trish felt more at peace than she had at any time in her life.

"I've got a special present for my best man," Logan said as they walked from the Clerk's office.

"What is it?" Fritz demanded.

"Just wait," Logan said, a hint of mischief in his voice.

They walked past the park, stopping for a brief swing, and then on down Chestnut Street to Logan's house.

"Here it is," he said.

"Here's what?" Fritz asked. "It's your house."

"Our house, now," Trish cautioned.

They had moved most of their belongings into the house during the previous weekend and Trish was hopeful that Fritz would have an easier time with this move than with the previous one.

"Unh-unh," Logan corrected. "It's *Fritz's* house."

"What do you mean?" Trish asked.

He pulled from his pocket a piece of paper, which he unfurled in front of her.

"Let me see," Fritz ordered, crowding between them.

"It's the deed to the house," Logan said. "I had it transferred to Fritz."

"Wow! So, I own this place now?" Fritz asked, and at Logan's nodded reply, he began to race—arms outstretched—from one end of the yard to another, checking out his land.

"Why did you do that?" Trish asked, surprised into blurting out the question.

"I actually did it before you even agreed to be my wife," Logan explained. "I wanted Fritz to have the security that you've looked for. No matter what happens to any of us, he has a home."

"Oh, Logan, you've done so much already—" Trish began, thinking of Logan's resignation from the force.

"I'm a different person, now," Logan interrupted gently. "You've shown me the way to let go of the cynicism and the shame about my brother that were keeping me on the force and keeping people at a distance. I never would have thought I would marry, Trish. That I would have a son like Fritz. That I would have a business as a consultant and wear a suit. That I would welcome my brother back when he gets out of prison. That I would be so happy."

They kissed and their arms entwined about

each other. Soon they were lost in the sensations and urges that only two people deeply in love could feel.

"Hey, guys!" Fritz interrupted. "If this is my house, do I get to decide what we have for dinner tonight?"

Logan laughed, breaking away from Trish.

"I didn't realize the problems I would create," he said mock-seriously.

"That's okay," Trish said, smiling at her husband. "It's going to give a whole new meaning to the motherly command of clean your room."

"Guys? Do I get to decide?" Fritz asked, impatient with their lovey-dovey looks and talk. Enough was enough.

"Only if it's pizza," Trish said. "Now let's go inside *your* house and call Cheese-to-Please."

"Yippee!" Fritz cried as he hurtled himself through the front entrance.

"Wait! Fritz, no running in the house!" Trish exclaimed, heading for the door after her son.

"Wait one minute, Mrs. Powell," Logan said, grabbing her arm. "There's something the husband is supposed to do."

He picked her up, bringing her into the safety of his arms, exuberantly kissing her. Then, as she giggled with delight, he walked in easy strides to the front door, kicked it gently open and brought them both into their new home.

*   *   *   *   *

Americana HEROES
AGAINST ALL ODDS

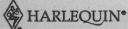 **HARLEQUIN®**   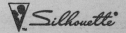 *Silhouette®*

Please address questions and book requests to: Harlequin Reader Service U.S.: 3010 Walden Ave.,
P.O. Box 1325, Buffalo, NY 14269 CAN.: P.O. Box 609, Fort Erie, Ont. L2A 5X3   PAHGEN

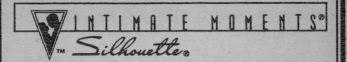

If you've got the time...
We've got the
INTIMATE MOMENTS

Passion. Suspense. Desire. Drama.
Enter a world that's larger than life,
where men and women overcome life's
greatest odds for the ultimate prize: love.
Nonstop excitement is closer than you
think...in Silhouette Intimate Moments!

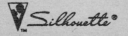

SIMGEN99

FOUR UNIQUE SERIES
FOR EVERY WOMAN YOU ARE...

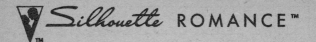

These entertaining, tender and involving love stories
celebrate the spirit of pure romance.

Desire features strong heroes and spirited heroines
who come together in a highly passionate,
emotionally powerful and always provocative read.

Silhouette® SPECIAL EDITION®

For every woman who dreams of life, love and family,
these are the romances in which she makes
her dreams come true.

Dive into the pages of Intimate Moments and experience
adventure and excitement in these complex
and dramatic romances.

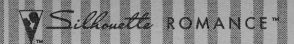